THE
DIFFERENCE
BETWEEN
YOU
AND
ME

THE
DIFFERENCE
BETWEEN
YOU
AND
ME

madeleine george

viking

An Imprint of Penguin Group (USA) Inc.

viking
Published by Penguin Group
Penguin Group (USA) Inc., 345 Hudson Street, New York, New York 10014, U.S.A.
Penguin Group (Canada), 90 Eglinton Avenue East, Suite 700, Toronto, Ontario, Canada
M4P 2Y3 (a division of Pearson Penguin Canada Inc.)
Penguin Books Ltd, 80 Strand, London WC2R 0RL, England
Penguin Ireland, 25 St Stephen's Green, Dublin 2, Ireland (a division of Penguin Books Ltd)
Penguin Group (Australia), 250 Camberwell Road, Camberwell, Victoria 3124, Australia
(a division of Pearson Australia Group Pty Ltd)
Penguin Books India Pvt Ltd, 11 Community Centre, Panchsheel Park, New Delhi – 110 017, India
Penguin Group (NZ), 67 Apollo Drive, Rosedale, Auckland 0632, New Zealand
(a division of Pearson New Zealand Ltd.)
Penguin Books (South Africa) (Pty) Ltd, 24 Sturdee Avenue, Rosebank,
Johannesburg 2196, South Africa

Penguin Books Ltd, Registered Offices: 80 Strand, London WC2R 0RL, England

First published in 2012 by Viking, a member of Penguin Group (USA) Inc.

1   3   5   7   9   10   8   6   4   2

Copyright © Madeleine George, 2012
All rights reserved

LIBRARY OF CONGRESS CATALOGING-IN-PUBLICATION DATA
George, Madeleine.
The difference between you and me / by Madeleine George.
p. cm.
Summary: School outsider Jesse, a lesbian, is having secret trysts with Emily,
the popular student council vice president, but when they find themselves on
opposite sides of a major issue and Jesse becomes more involved with a student activist,
they are forced to make a difficult decision.
ISBN 978-0-670-01128-5 (hardcover)
[1. Lesbians—Fiction. 2. Protest movements—Fiction. 3. High schools—Fiction.
4. Schools—Fiction.] I. Title.
PZ7.G293346Di 2012   [Fic]—dc23   2011012192

Printed in U.S.A.   Set in Century Light

All rights reserved. No part of this book may be reproduced, scanned, or distributed in any printed
or electronic form without permission. Please do not participate in or encourage piracy of
copyrighted materials in violation of the author's rights. Purchase only authorized editions.

THE
DIFFERENCE
BETWEEN
YOU
AND
ME

THE NOLAW MANIFESTO

Demanding
JUSTICE NOW!
for All
Weirdos, Freaks,
Queer Kids, Revolutionaries,
Nerds, Dweebs,
Misfits, Loudmouths,
Rapunzels Trapped in Their Towers,
Trolls Trapped under Their Bridges,
Animals Abused by Their Masters,
DETENTIONITES,
Monsters,
and Saints.
By the
**National Organization to Liberate
All Weirdos,**
or

Point I.
NORMALCY IS DEATH!

Point II.
Weirdness Is Life!

Point III.

Weirdos must **COME OUT!** The more weirdos who **COME OUT!** as weird, queer, freakish, nerdy, dweeby, loud-mouthed, or otherwise unfit for quote unquote "normal society," the closer we will come to **TEARING DOWN** quote unquote "normal society" and replacing it with a beautiful **KINGDOM OF WEIRDNESS** in which all Weirdos will be free to express every part of themselves in every part of school or the bus or work or church or temple or mosque or wherever it is they want to go. The **KINGDOM OF WEIRDNESS** will be a paradise of freedom on earth in which joy and happiness and clean forests and other unbesmirched kinds of nature reign and no one judges anyone else and eventually everyone will see how **VASTLY SUPERIOR** Weirdness is to quote unquote "normalcy" and quote unquote "normalcy" will wither away.

Point IV.
JUDGMENTAL PEOPLE SUCK!

Point V.

Even before the Dawn of the new **KINGDOM OF WEIRDNESS**, Weirdos, Freaks, and Queers must **DEMAND JUSTICE!** We must **DEMAND** to be recognized as Legitimate by quote unquote "normal society." We must make "Yeah? So what?" our total slogan. We must say it a thousand times a day until quote unquote "normal society" shrugs their shoulders at us and stops trying to make us Conform to their Strangulating Laws and Conventionalisms. We must **DEMAND** that they Leave Us Alone even if they don't grant us full human rights.

Point VI.

We Demand

for all Weirdos, Freaks, Queers,
Other Oppressed People et cetera!!!

FULL HUMAN RIGHTS INCLUDE:

The right to wear WHATEVER CLOTHES WE WANT, WHENEVER WE WANT TO WEAR THEM.
The right to **MAKE OUT** with **WHOMEVER WE WANT** TO regardless of RACE, COLOR, CREED, CLASS, NEIGHBORHOOD OF ORIGIN, **EXTRACURRICULAR AFFILIATION**, or **GENDER**.
The right to use WHICHEVER BATHROOM WE FEEL LIKE USING and not to have to hold it until we can sneak into the one faculty bathroom that is not possibly full of abusive idiots waiting to **ABUSE AND INSULT US FOR ABSOLUTELY NO REASON!!!**

1

Jesse

Jesse is in the sophomore hall girls' bathroom, the farthest stall from the door, one huge, scuffed fisherman's boot propped up on the toilet seat so she can balance her backpack on her knee and rifle through it. She's looking for the masking tape that she totally, totally put in here this morning, she's positive, she has a perfect picture-memory of swiping it out of the designated masking-tape cubby in her mother's rolltop desk in the den and dropping it into her backpack, the big pocket, right here she totally put it here where is it where is it the bell's about to ring—

The plan is to wait until the pep rally is called and then paper the entire school with the latest draft of her manifesto in one lightning-quick, thirty-eight-minute blitz while the rest of the student body is penned in the gym bleating and baaing like the sheep they are. It's a sweet, satisfying plan, but it can't begin to happen without masking tape. Tape tape tape tape—Jesse digs deeper, feels around frantically in the backpack's gummy innards.

And the bell rings and the announcement comes over the PA—"annual spirit assembly being held at this time in the gym, all students proceed to the gym at this time"— and Jesse whispers, "Shit!" and starts to sweat.

The door swings open, admitting a blast of hallway-at-passing-time noise, and a clutch of girls come in, mid-giggling-conversation. In her stall, Jesse freezes, presses back against the cool cinder-block wall.

"Um, I mean, no *way*? It's *obviously* a lie?"

Through the sliver of space between stall door and stall wall, Jesse makes out a blur of blonde as the girls arrange themselves in front of the long mirror over the sinks. One of the girls is explaining something to the others in a tone that implies that they are totally stupid. She says every sentence with an implied *"I mean, duh"* after it.

"She can *say* they hooked up? She can go around *telling* everyone they hooked up if she wants people to think she's a total *slut*? But there is no *way* they hooked up, just because I *know* that guy and that guy is *impossible* to get with."

"Impossible," one of the other girls echoes, and giggles a little.

Jesse's knee begins to bounce. Her jaw tightens. If they were just here to pee it would be one thing, but these girls are settling in for a full hair-and-makeup session in front of the mirrors. Prepping for pepping. *Go go GO!* Jesse shouts at them telepathically. She has to be clear of this bathroom by no later than one minute before first period, otherwise—

"Like, remember at Dylan's party how hard I had to work to get him to hook up with me?" the first girl continues. "I practically had to slip him a roofie, remember?"

"A roofie." The second girl giggles again vaguely.

"Remember I practically had to slip him a roofie and like beat him over the head with a club and like drag him back to my *lair* to get him to hook up with me at Dylan's party? So there is *no* way he got with Lauren. If *I* have to go through all that just to get him? And she's like a total barking *dog*? I'm sorry, I just don't believe it."

"But why would she lie about it?" A third girl speaks, and Jesse's heart stops, briefly—just pulls into a parking space and pauses. It's Emily.

"I don't see why she'd spread a rumor about her own sluttiness," Emily continues evenly, reasonably. Emily always sounds like that, like she's making a point that everyone else is guaranteed to agree with.

"Uh, to seem less ugly, obviously?" First Girl sneers. Second Girl giggles: *Duh.*

"I don't see where her lying about being slutty would make anybody think she's less ugly," Emily says. "It doesn't make sense." Jesse can picture her shrugging her I-guess-there's-nothing-more-to-say-about-it shrug, perfect round shoulders in their soft J.Crew sweater bobbing up and down, a smooth, case-closed bounce.

But is it the J.Crew sweater today? Jesse's curiosity rises in her like a blush to her cheeks. Is it the pink one with the fake pearl buttons? Or maybe the black V-neck she wears over the white button-down? It could be the Vander High hoodie—it is spirit assembly today, after all, and Emily *loves* spirit. If Jesse were smart she wouldn't move a muscle until these girls were gone, but she can't help herself. Even a tiny slice of Emily is worth seeing.

Carefully, soundlessly, Jesse brings her big, galumphy fisherman's boot down off the toilet seat, cradling her backpack to her chest to keep it from slipping out of her grasp and crashing to the floor. She hunkers down and leans against the stall door, pressing her eye to the cold gap between door and wall. Emily is right there, not even three feet away, her back to Jesse, slim, denim hip jutted out to one side, gathering her long, thick, strawberry blonde hair into a single rope rising straight up off the top of her head. Quick as a samurai, she twists the hair-rope around and around, then spreads her left hand wide as a starfish with a ponytail holder stretched around her fingers, open to its widest width, then pulls the hair through the holder once, twice, then splits it into two hanks and yanks the whole thing tight. She tips her head first to one side, then the other, assessing the ponytail's height, form, and placement in the mirror. It's a move Jesse has seen her do dozens of times, but she could watch it a thousand more and never get tired of it. It's like watching a Cirque du Soleil gymnast flip ten times through the air and stick the landing.

"You guys, whatever about Lauren, we have to not be late right now." Emily's voice is clear and judgment free, brightened only by enthusiasm. "We have to get seats by the back wall if we want to help hold the banner."

As Emily steps out of viewing range, Jesse strains against the stall door, trying to keep her in her sights as she moves. It's this pressure, probably, plus the shift in her weight as she goes to set her backpack down gently on the floor, that causes the rickety, worthless stall door to un-latch and fly open, sending Jesse sprawling face-forward onto the floor right at the girls' feet, her backpack beneath her and her big green boots kicked out behind her.

The girls squeal. Jesse grunts.

"Oh my God," shrieks First Girl, "oh my God oh my God!"

"Sorry," Jesse mumbles, facedown. She hauls herself not terribly gracefully to her feet, afraid to look up, afraid to meet Emily's eye.

"Um, excuse me," First Girl says, her initial shock mel-lowing into casual contempt. "Don't you know this is the *girls'* room?"

Second Girl giggles abruptly, then stops.

Ocean roars, distantly, in Jesse's ears.

She lifts her head and looks straight at them. Emily is

in the center of the trio (it *is* the Vander High hoodie—navy blue with the big yellow V on the left breast), her arms crossed over her chest, summery head tipped quizzically to one side, flanked by her two virtually identical friends. It's like there's a mirror Emily on either side of the real Emily: hoodie hoodie hoodie, jeans jeans jeans, ponytail ponytail ponytail. In the center of the triptych, Emily stands looking at Jesse with terrible blankness, a perfectly placid unrecognition. It's like she's never seen Jesse before and doesn't much care that she's seeing her now.

Jesse turns to First Girl, on Emily's left. First Girl's eyes and the corners of her mouth are merry with evil. Jesse feels her fists clenching involuntarily.

"I'm sorry, what?" Jesse says. The calm she tries to maintain in these moments is fraying, and this comes out sounding a little bit like a threat.

First Girl takes it as one. She lengthens her neck defensively, tosses her blondeness over one shoulder, and repeats, "I said, this is the *girls'* room."

Every time this happens—and it happens to Jesse a couple of times a week, in the bathroom at the library, the locker room at the pool, Friendly's, Starbucks, the ladies' fitting room at the hideous disgusting hateful Fashion Bug, at school, at school, all the time at school—there comes a moment in the confrontation when it is Jesse's turn to speak. Sometimes, especially with confused adults, she says politely, "I know, I *am* a girl." Sometimes she gets it together and educates the person: "There are lots of different ways to be a girl." Sometimes, if she's having a bad day, she says, "Yes, it *is* the girls' room, are you lost?"

But today, with Emily looking at her, just looking at her and not saying anything in her defense, Jesse comes up empty. She opens her mouth but nothing comes out.

First Girl gasps a little and grips Emily's arm. "Oh my God, you guys," she says, "she was watching us in there!"

"Ew gross!" Second Girl wails.

Jesse's heart starts to pound. Her tongue thickens in her half-open mouth.

"She must have been, like, waiting for us to take our shirts off or something," First Girl hisses. "Oh my God, disgusting. Oh my God, I feel so gross right now."

Jesse turns back to Emily, searching her face for anything—backup; sympathy; defense; some big, distracting move that would steal their attention away from Jesse. But there's nothing there.

Over the PA comes the final announcement: "One minute remaining in passing period. All students proceed to the gym for spirit assembly at this time."

Now Emily springs into action. "Okay, you guys, come on, let it go," she says in a light, coaxy-friendly way to her friends. "We cannot be late for assembly today."

First Girl turns a fake-sympathetic face on Emily. "Oh,

Em, that's so *nice* that you're trying to protect your boy-friend. You should stay and hang out with her, look, she totally wants you."

Instantly, Jesse looks down at the floor. Her face cannot sustain examination for traces of lust for Emily Miller—it might be there, even if she's trying to suppress it with every ounce of her energy.

"Oh, stop it," Emily says, exasperated—the way you'd speak to a pesky child. "I'm leaving." Emily turns and holds open the bathroom door, a wordless command. Despite herself, Jesse thinks, *You're not even going to look at me one more time?*

First Girl sighs. "Whatever, you're such a control freak, Em." She gives her hair a final check in the mirror. "Bye, dyke!" she chirps cheerfully over her shoulder as she leaves, pulling Second Girl along with her.

As Emily turns to walk out the door she meets Jesse's eye for a fraction of a second. Her expression is scrunched-up and confusing, part *Sorry* and part *What can you do?* and part *I know, this is so dumb* and part *Hey, it's no big deal!* A pity mishmash. This is not at all what Jesse wants. Jesse wants *These girls are titanic mega-idiots and I renounce their friendship as of this moment and I'll meet you in our usual spot at the library this afternoon and totally,* totally *make it up to you.* Jesse takes a step forward as if to stop Emily, but even as she moves, Emily lets the door fall shut behind her.

A moment of quiet.

Jesse realizes that her heart is pounding.

In the mirror above the row of sinks, Jesse looks back at herself. She doesn't look like much. Dark, angry eyes, messy thatched-roof haircut the color and texture of straw, clenched fists, square shoulders, ringer tee, cargo pants, fisherman's boots.

Why do you have to wear those boots? Wyatt asks her almost every time he sees her. *If you have to wear boots, fine, but why giant, loose, flopping, knee-high rubber boots that make you look like you just got off work at the slaughterhouse?*

They make me feel solid, Jesse almost always says. *I like to feel planted when I walk.*

Crazy, Wyatt says to her. *Rebel Without a Cause.*

From outside the door in the hallway comes a muffled blast of static, like a blip from the sound track of the moon landing—far away, but close enough that it makes Jesse's neck stiffen, wild-animal style. Blast of static means Snediker's coming, walkie-talkie live and crackling, clipped to the lower pocket of her blazer.

Ms. Snediker, dean of students, is an iron marshmallow. She's short and stout, pink cheeked and gray haired, and she rarely blinks. She always wears a flower-print dress with a skinny belt straining to stay clasped around her high, tight basketball of a middle. In her yearbook picture every year she poses, unsmiling, plump arms hanging stiffly by her sides, beside the wall of mug shots she keeps in her office, photos of kids she's caught violating handbook rules or trying to sneak off campus during school hours. She calls this her "Hall of Shame." She has a small, nasal voice that she never raises and that in no way matches the things she uses it to say: "busted," frequently; "suspended," whenever she gets the chance; and sometimes, on her luckiest days, "expelled." Snediker is the Terminator. Snediker is coming.

Jesse is trapped.

The bathroom sweep is Snediker's specialty. Out the door would mean running right into her meaty arms—a one-way ticket to disciplinary. But back into the stall is the fool's direction: Snediker keeps a long-handled retractable mirror tool on her person at all times that she snaps out to its full length during bathroom sweeps to check under stall doors for toilet-crouchers. Anyway, the boots make crouching impractical. Jesse scans the bathroom desperately for an exit strategy, molten panic bubbling in her chest.

High up by the ceiling above the radiator unit is a long, narrow portal window, the kind you push out to open. It's too high and too small for anyone but a moron or a superhero to try to squeeze through. It's decoration, not an escape hatch. It's not part of a realistic plan. Jesse tugs her backpack over her shoulders and clambers up onto the radiator unit to reach it.

In her mind, Jesse hears Wyatt, calm and firm: *Absolutely not. Absolutely not, have you finally, completely lost your mind? First of all it's as high as your head, you'll never get up there. Second of all it's as wide as a Pop-Tart, you'll never fit through it. Third of all what are you gonna do if you do get through,* fly? *It's fourteen feet down to the ground and* then *you're trapped in the inner courtyard, where do you think you're gonna go from there?*

Jesse thinks about Emily's scrunched-up, confused expression as she left the bathroom: *Sorry, sort of!*

She unhooks the window latch and punches the swivel frame out—it opens about twenty inches, not nearly enough for her to squeeze through. She grips the sharp sill with both hands and, sending all her strength to her arms and shoulders, *jumps!* up and manages to wedge herself into the window frame. Her head and shoulders are crammed through, but her whole back three-quarters is still dangling inside the bathroom. The rounded tiptoes of her fisherman's boots just graze the radiator cover now—not enough contact there for leverage—and her shoulders are so squeezed she can't wriggle another inch forward. She tries to reverse course but the backpack, fat with manifestos, has her stuck.

Behind Jesse, a blast of static. In front of her: a square of gravel, a dwindling horizon of possibilities.

Jesse hears the squeal of the bathroom door swinging wide on its hinges, feels the rush of air around her that is suddenly sucked through the room when it opens.

And then, Snediker's high, mirthless whine:

"Busted."

2

Emily

With me, it's about the person. I don't believe in labels. I think people should be free to do whatever they want with whoever they want. Some people might say I'm bisexual and the only reason I *wouldn't* say that is because I don't believe in labels of any kind. I feel so grateful to be growing up today, when things are so much more free than they used to be. Nowadays people can just be who they are, they don't have to define themselves in words.

I'm very tolerant of all different kinds of differences. I was the one who *proposed* the Diversity Circus event to student council last year and headed the committee that organized it and found us a venue for it off campus and figured out how to rent the pony for pony rides and it was a ton of work but P.S.? We made a huge pile of money on it— it was one of our top three biggest moneymaking events of the year for student council, after the Fall Formal and the Lasagna Supper, which are always the biggest events of the year and which are traditions, so they're guaranteed to make money. Diversity Circus was a brand-new event on the student council calendar and *still* it came in third for revenue for the year, and we used part of the money we made on it to bring in a speaker from the national office of GLSEN, which is the Gay, Lesbian and Straight Education Network, an awesome organization, and even though I didn't have time to attend that event, I did book the room for it and I had a big part in making it happen and I heard that it went really well. Lots of people came.

One of the things I love best about our school is that it's such a diverse place. I have one friend who has a small hand from birth and one other friend who's a Muslim—she wears a head scarf and everything. At some schools those people might get teased or made to feel unwelcome, but at our school those kids are as welcome as any normal kids. I'm really, really proud of that. As vice president of student council, I feel personally responsible for making our school such a welcoming, diverse place. To me, that's one of the most important parts of my job.

But unfortunately, that's partly why my personal life has to be so complicated. As vice president of student council I have a responsibility to be sort of the public face of the school. When I walk around school, or around town, even, I don't just represent myself, I represent the entire student body. That's why I don't just get to do whatever I want whenever I want to. It's like, if I wanted to get drunk

THE DIFFERENCE BETWEEN **YOU** AND **ME**

on a Saturday night and go joyriding in my parents' car—tons of kids do this, I've seen them—I can't, because I have to think about my public persona and my responsibility to the school. If I wanted to cut class and go do some shoplifting at the mall, or smoke cigarettes in the parking lot, or not do my homework, or do any different kind of rule-breaking thing that other kids do for fun without even thinking about it, I can't, because for a person with a public persona like me, there are consequences. If I want to get sort of involved with Jesse Halberstam in any way, I have to really, really think about what that could do not just to me, not just to Michael, but to the entire school. It's a serious responsibility.

The problem with Michael isn't even Michael, it's that we've been together for so long. Michael and I have known each other since we were born, and we've been going out since eighth grade, which is really too young to start dating someone, I realize now that I'm older. Our parents let it happen because our moms are *best*-best friends, they've known each other forever, since before college even. They love that we're together, our dads love that we're together, everyone in school loves that we're together. We're the proverbial perfect couple. Sometimes I feel like I don't know what would happen to this town if we broke up—so many people have so much invested in our relationship. I mean, I do, too—I love him, we've shared so much over the years, and we know each other so well. We've grown up together.

We're practically brother and sister. Which is the problem. You shouldn't go out with someone who feels like a member of your family.

Jesse Halberstam does not feel like a member of my family. Sometimes she doesn't even feel like a member of my species. She's so . . . I don't know, I can't explain her. She's a mess. She cuts her own hair with a Swiss Army Knife. She picks the mosquito bites on her arms until they bleed. She wears those unspeakable rubber boots. Half the time when she talks I don't understand a word she's saying, and the other half the time she's saying something totally bonkers about how we have to, like, smash society and live in its ruins like futuristic barbarian cave people or whatever. I just tune her out when she talks like that. If I actually listened to her theories about the world, I'd have to conclude she was mentally insane. But most of the time I don't have to listen to her theories because she's not talking, she's kissing me.

She's an incredibly good kisser. I don't . . . I can't explain it. It's not something I can explain.

When me and Michael kiss, it's like I'm making out with a cut cantaloupe. He is the wettest, squishiest kisser on the planet. He's so cute from a distance, you know, he's such a good-looking guy, like a male model practically, but then when he goes to kiss me it's like all the muscles in his face go slack and his lips get all spongy and loose and he opens his loose face and sort of lays his spongy lips all over me and drools his melon-juice spit into my mouth. It's horrible. I don't mean to criticize him, I'm sure lots of other girls would think he was a totally amazing kisser, it's just . . . sometimes I have to pretend he's getting too powerful and intense and I push him off me, but really I'm pushing him off me because he's getting too disgusting. One time he kissed me so wetly for so long that his drool actually dripped down my neck. Sometimes right when I'm about to fall asleep, I suddenly remember the feeling of his spit sliding down my neck and I wake up so fast and hard my heart starts pounding in my chest and it takes me, like, hours to fall back to sleep.

It's not his fault. He just gets really excited, like a dog. Like a sweet, slobbery golden retriever.

When Jesse Halberstam kisses me, she's really focused and really intense. She puts her hands on the sides of my face to hold me where she wants me, or she winds her fingers up in my hair and tugs it tight, and somehow, just by the way she touches me, she makes my mouth open, she makes my eyes close, she makes me breathe faster and faster until I feel dizzy and I think I might black out. Sometimes when she's kissing me, I swear to God, the edges of my body melt and I become sort of part of her. Sometimes when she kisses me I forget my own name.

But then when I go home again I remember. I know who I am. I'm Emily Miller.

Jesse

The frozen veggie burritos are in the oven. The prewashed organic lettuce is in the salad bowl. The radio is on in the den: *All Things Considered*—familiar, muted horn salute, the blurred murmur of NPR voices. Jesse is on one side of the kitchen table, and her parents are on the other.

"What is this, a show trial?" Jesse demands. "A firing squad?"

"This is not a firing squad," her father says gently. Jesse's father has a beard and a bald spot, half-glasses, and a permanent, ever-changing sweater vest. His voice is rich and resonant as a cello solo; he smells of Rooibos tea.

"When the firing squad starts, you won't have to ask," her mother says sharply. Jesse's mother has super-short, bright white hair—growing in finally after the chemo last spring—and little round John Lennon glasses. Her arms are crossed over her favorite T-shirt, which is green with big white letters that read: DARFUR IS HAPPENING NOW.

She smells of soap and Wite-Out. She almost always keeps one eyebrow raised in rueful disbelief.

"This is a *conversation*," Jesse's father says, "about what happened at school today."

"I don't really feel like having a conversation about what happened at school today." Jesse shrugs.

"Well, you're gonna," snaps her mother. Jesse's father lays a restraining hand lightly on his wife's arm.

"Sweetheart," he says to Jesse, "it's not that we don't respect your feelings about pep rallies—"

"Pep rallies revolt me," Jesse interrupts.

"And we respect that. You have every right to those feelings. But handling those feelings by crawling through a bathroom window—"

"Unsuccessfully," her mother points out.

"Handling those perfectly legitimate, valid feelings by crawling through a bathroom window, sweetheart, is a maladaptive coping strategy that—"

"Shrinkydink." Jesse cuts him off.

"I'm sorry, I'll rephrase." Her father has agreed not to use terms from his family therapy practice with his daughter except in extreme emotional emergencies. "By choosing this way of handling your feelings you . . . you complicated things, you made things harder on yourself, you—"

"You screwed up," her mother interrupts, impatient. "Is this NYU-bound behavior? This bathroom-window Keystone Kops routine?"

"Fran." Now Jesse's father lays his hand on his wife's shoulder, but she shrugs it off.

"I'm pissed, Arthur, I don't want to be calmed down, I want to be angry!"

"I hear you, but—"

"What were you *thinking*?" Fran stares her daughter down. "I hate to have to say that, it's such a parenting cliché, but what on earth was going through your *mind* at that moment?"

Jesse takes a deep breath and presents her case.

"Pep rallies revolt me. I refuse to attend them and in this quote unquote free country I shouldn't have to. I can't believe I have to explain this to you guys! Pep rallies are fascist demonstrations of loyalty and I am not loyal to my school. I hate my school. I'm the opposite of loyal to it. If I wouldn't end up in jail, I would blow it up."

"If you wouldn't end up in jail, blowing it up wouldn't be much of a principled statement," Fran observes. She's a lawyer; she can't resist a counterargument.

"I'm curious about why we're talking about the violent destruction of property all of a sudden," asks Arthur.

"Because apparently your daughter is an incipient terrorist!" Fran shouts, turning on her husband. "And not, I might add, a particularly competent one."

Jesse looks down at her lap, stung.

"I'm sorry." Jesse's mother flushes red. She gives Jesse a look of sincere apology. "I'm sorry, honey. I'm sure if you

THE DIFFERENCE BETWEEN **YOU** AND **ME**

were a terrorist, you'd make a wonderful one."

"Okay, so what I'd really like right now," interjects Arthur again, "is to turn away from talking about terrorism and violence and move on to talking about the actual consequences of Jesse's actions today. Is that okay with everyone?"

The women in his life nod.

"All right. So what exactly is 'alternative' about this Alternative Suspension Program?"

Jesse sighs. "You have to like, 'give back,' or whatever. They make you come in on Saturday morning and do chores. That way, you don't miss class and you benefit the school."

"Well," Fran says, "that seems reasonable enough. Maybe if you spend a little time giving back, next time you'll consider whether skipping a pep rally is really the best place to put your revolutionary energy."

"And sweetheart, think of this as an opportunity," Arthur offers. "You never know what's going to happen when you take on the establishment. You know your mother and I met in prison after a No Nukes demonstration."

"God I *know*," Jesse sighs exasperatedly, "*please* do not tell me the story again and you *always* say prison and it was *not* prison, it was a holding area in the gym at the university!"

"Still," Fran says. She smiles sweetly, almost shyly, at her husband.

Arthur strokes the back of his wife's hand with two fingers. "They booked us one right after the other," he says dreamily. "I stood behind her in line at the fingerprint station they had set up on this little card table under the basketball hoop. I was there with some of my buddies from the Men Finding Power Through Peace Coalition, and there she was, all alone. She came there all by herself because she saw something wrong in the world and wanted to make it right. And I thought, 'What a brave person.' And then I thought, 'They're going to press her fingers down in the ink and then they're going to press *my* fingers down in the ink right afterward. It's almost like we'll be holding hands.'"

Arthur picks up Fran's hand and kisses the back of it. She rolls her eyes at him a little, but she's still smiling.

"Are you guys about to make out?" Jesse demands.

"We might," her father says, not taking his eyes off his wife. "We might make out."

"You know"—Jesse gets up from the table—"it's fine that you guys are heterosexual, your lifestyle choice is none of my business, but I don't see why you have to rub my face in it all the time. This house is totally gender-oppressive and I'm sick of it. I'm here, I'm queer—"

"We're used to it," her mother sighs.

✷ ✷ ✷

"Typical," Wyatt sighs on the phone when Jesse explains what has happened.

Jesse is lying on her bed with her head hanging off the end and her sock feet up on the pillow, talking to her best friend. Since Wyatt left school in the middle of last year to be homeschooled by his aromatherapist-slash-animal-psychic mom, he basically does nothing but read books about finance and wait for Jesse to get home from school so they can talk. "Nice job, getting yourself thrown into jail on the *one* day you were going to come run interference for me with Howard."

"It's not jail, it's Alternative Suspension."

"Whatever. You don't seem particularly devastated not to be spending your Saturday with me and Mr. Willette."

Howard Willette is Wyatt's father. He and Wyatt's mother got divorced ten years ago, shortly after he accepted Christ as his personal savior—apparently, evangelical Christianity and aromatherapy proved to be incompatible belief systems. Four years ago, Howard married Louise, an even more conservative Christian than he is, and moved to Stonington, two towns away, to Wyatt's great relief. But he still insists on honoring his monthly court-mandated coffee date with Wyatt, even though they have trouble exchanging even the most basic pleasantries without arguing. (Wyatt is a card-carrying member of the Atheist Alliance International. And the Queer Libertarian

League.) For a while now, Jesse has been coming with Wyatt on these coffee dates to distract them both and cut the tension with dumb jokes. She saves up G-rated punch lines and wholesome anecdotes about heroic pets all month long to use as subject-changers.

"I am *so* devastated. I'm totally devastated not to be there with you on Saturday. I have, like, three great new knock-knocks all ready to go!"

"What were you doing hiding in the bathroom anyway? That's amateur stuff—you *know* how Snediker is with bathroom sweeps."

"No, I know, it's so dumb, I wasn't supposed to be in there, or I was, but I was only supposed to be in there for a *second*. I just—something happened and I got distracted."

Jesse wishes—so much wishes—she could tell Wyatt about the encounter with Emily today. For almost a year now she's been managing to keep Emily a secret. Wyatt doesn't even know she exists. It's been excruciating— almost impossible—concealing this huge part of her life, but it seems even more impossible to start telling him about it now. How would she even bring it up? It's been going on for so long and it's so terrible, what Jesse's agreed to. There's no way Wyatt would let it continue if he knew.

"Oh, something happened?" Wyatt is sympathetic. "Something digestive?"

"Ew, no!" Jesse cries. "Gross! I just, it's so dumb, I had masking tape in my bag and I was trying to get it out so

I could put up my manifestos during the pep rally and I couldn't find it and then the bell rang and I was stuck there. That's all that happened."

Wyatt groans. "Not the manifestos! *That's* why you got thrown in jail, for those ridiculous manifestos? Beloved, when are you going to figure out that this little art project of yours is a colossal waste of time?"

Jesse breathes, wills herself to stay calm. This is the biggest point of contention between them. If she had been thinking straight, she would have made up a totally different story about getting busted and avoided having to discuss this with Wyatt for eight millionth time. But she was not thinking straight. She was distracted by making up a story about being distracted by something other than Emily Miller.

"Okay, first of all," Jesse says, forcing herself to stay cool, "they are not a 'little art project.' They are a series of serious political wake-up calls that I post around school because I'm trying to change things there and make the world a safer place for weirdos like you and me."

"I'm not—" Wyatt starts, but Jesse cuts him off.

"Yeah, yeah, you're not a weirdo, I know, and *second* of all, not that I want to miss our Howard date, I totally don't, but I do actually think it's worth getting thrown in jail for a cause you believe is important."

"Mm-hm," Wyatt murmurs. "Have you even started *The Fountainhead* yet?"

"I told you I'm not going to read that book. What is the *matter* with you that your idol is Ayn Rand, why can't you worship Cher or Judy Garland like any normal gay boy?"

"Because I don't have a low opinion of myself," Wyatt says breezily, and barrels on. "If you would read the book like I've asked you to politely, you would understand where you're going wrong. Miss Rand teaches us that egoism is the highest form of enlightenment. Trying to help other people is a twisted form of condescension, it makes people into dependent babies. And anyway, practically no one is smart enough to understand a 'serious political wake-up call' when they get one. The masses *want* to stay ignorant. And *those* masses? In *that* school? I've never seen a group of idiots so profoundly idiotic and so determined to stay that way. Why do you think I had to leave?"

"Because you couldn't get Rob Strong to stop tormenting you."

"Partly." From seventh grade until the beginning of last year, Wyatt was engaged in a long, slow, torturous war with Rob Strong, varsity wide receiver and king of auto shop. Something about Wyatt—his delicacy, his highly unusual outfits, the frustrating way he showed no fear even when he was about to get pounded—made Rob want to exterminate him. Eventually, it became clear that no amount of adult intervention was going to change their dynamic, and since neither Snediker nor Mr. Greil, the principal, was able to control Rob, Wyatt's mom gave into Wyatt's lifelong wish to be emancipated from school and pulled him, right at the beginning of ninth grade.

A lot of things had been changing in Jesse's world when Wyatt left. Her mother had just started cancer treatments, and Jesse was spending more time alone at home. And with Wyatt gone at school, she was alone a lot there, too. Since seventh grade, she had had almost all her classes with Wyatt. They had walked to school together almost every morning and hung out almost every afternoon. When Wyatt's mom took him out, it felt to Jesse like Wyatt had been her clothes, in a way, and now that he was gone she was walking around naked, exposed and alone in the halls of school.

It was then that she started working seriously on her manifestos. Pretty soon after that, she accidentally kissed Emily Miller for the first time.

It would have been impossible to keep Emily a secret if Wyatt had been there in school with her. But it didn't take long for him to lose interest in Vander after he stopped going there every day. In the beginning, he still asked about whether Mr. DiNapoli had worn the red loose baggy sweater or the blue loose baggy sweater that day, or if they'd had the excellent Tater Tots in the à la carte line at the cafeteria, or what kind of polo shirt Justin Hasaki-Bernstein had had on in Spanish. But after only a few weeks, Wyatt started to act like the people Jesse was talking about were characters in some foreign-language soap opera, remote and unreal, instead of the actual flesh-and-blood humans who populated her real life, all day, every day.

This year, Wyatt doesn't even know half of Jesse's teachers. He's not reading *Bleak House* or *Their Eyes Were Watching God*. He doesn't care about the new schedule change that turns either fourth or fifth period into a long lunch every third day, confusing the hell out of the entire school. When Jesse complains about the new schedule, Wyatt sighs and says things like, "It's a shame when little things have to take up so much of your time and attention." He doesn't get that this schedule change is not a little thing—not if you have hideously un-fun trigonometry and hideously dull Foundations of Western Culture during fourth and fifth periods (Jesse does).

One thing that hasn't changed is their favorite afternoon activity. One of Wyatt's main hobbies—second only to following the stock market online—is the construction of what he calls "sartorial personae," costumey outfits built around interesting pieces of clothing he finds at Rose's Turn, a dark little hole-in-the-wall thrift shop tucked under the train bridge down on Route 9. Wyatt will find a curious garment (a plaid blazer, say) and gradually build an iconic outfit around it, adding other items and accessories (lime green slacks, argyle socks, a salmon-colored polyester button-down shirt, gold Scorpio-sign medallion), and refining the effect until he's worked out a com-

THE DIFFERENCE BETWEEN YOU AND ME

plete persona (Golf Course Lady-Killer). Then this will become his uniform for a while—he'll wear it every day for a few weeks or months, until he gets bored with it and starts building another persona. Last year he spent time as 1960s Corporate Executive, Ex-Marine, Punk-Rock Street Thug, Mozart in *Amadeus*, and Friendly Grandpa, feeling them out until they were just right, then abandoning them. Lately he's been working on a sort of gay Hugh Hefner look—velveteen smoking jacket with a cigarette burn in the sleeve, ascot, fake-silk pajama bottoms, Isotoner slippers.

As long as they've been friends, Jesse has been going with him to Rose's Turn at least once a week, usually on Wednesday afternoons, since Marla, the college girl who works the register on Wednesdays, is super chill and lets them take an unlimited number of items into the dressing room at one time. Jesse has even found a few choice items for herself on certain Wednesdays, though Wyatt rarely approves of her selections. The best thing she ever found was an insanely awesome light blue tuxedo from the '70s—ruffled satin shirt, lapels as wide as surfboards, satin racing stripe down the side of each leg, and flappingly huge bell-bottom pants—so wide that her fisherman's boots fit easily inside. "I cannot permit you to pair those boots with that pantsuit," Wyatt had said at the time. "The boots or the pants alone are bad enough, but together they are an abomination in the sight of God."

"These pants were made for these boots," Jesse had argued. "That's why they call them boot cut!"

"I just wish you could spend your unique, brilliant energy in a more productive way," Wyatt continues now. "There are a few very extraordinary people in the world—of whom you and I are, of course, two—who strive for greatness in all things, and the way we do this is not by telling other people what to do, it's by setting an exceptional example and living brilliantly and getting everything we can get and ignoring everybody else. Anyway, that's what *I'm* going to do."

"Yes, I know you are."

"I'm going to get my GED by the end of this year and go to MIT and graduate a year early and start my own nanotech company and make microscopic cell phones that you implant in people's brain stems and be the youngest person ever to make the Forbes top ten wealthiest Americans list."

"Yes, I know."

"When I'm married to my gorgeous, brain-surgeon husband who loves to cook, you can come stay with us and our two chocolate labs at our beachfront house in Malibu."

"Thanks."

"And I was thinking," Wyatt continues, serious now, as if he's given what he's about to say a great deal of thought, "there should be one room in our guesthouse that's specifically designed for you, and no one but you can stay there.

And we'll have, like, copies of all your favorite books on the shelves and a mini-fridge with all your favorite snacks in it, and you can come anytime you want to and stay as long as you want. If you don't have a job or if you drop out of college or something you can come stay there indefinitely."

"Thanks."

"For years, even. You can, like, live there. We'll be so happy to have you."

"Thanks, Wy."

Wyatt sighs. Jesse pictures him rolling over onto his back on his—always—neatly made bed.

"Are you in your Hef-wear tonight?" she asks.

"Western," he says tonelessly. "I'm starting a new John Wayne thing. I can't believe I have to spend two hours with Howard without you there." Wyatt's bossy Ayn Rand voice has subsided. He sounds tired now, and small. "I wish you hadn't climbed out that idiot window."

"I'm sorry." Jesse feels a sick-guilty knot twist in her stomach. She can't stand the thought of Wyatt in his thrift-store Western wear sitting on that spindly metal chair at that wobbly round table in that dimly lit café, opposite coldhearted Howard, with no one to sit between them and absorb the bad energy.

"Hey," she offers hopefully, "how about I tell you the knock-knocks I was going to tell him, so you can distract him yourself if things gets tense."

"Okay," Wyatt says balefully. "Not that it'll help."

"Knock knock," Jesse begins.

"Who's there?"

"Interrupting cow."

"Interrupting—"

"MOO!" Jesse yells into the phone.

A pause. She can hear Wyatt rolling his eyes to the ceiling.

"Terrible," he says, smiling. "Terrible."

4

Emily

It was almost a year ago that I figured out that we should get corporate sponsorship for this year's Fall Formal. I was only student council secretary then, so I wasn't really involved in decision making, but I couldn't help taking mental notes during last year's dance and thinking about ways that it could be better. It's my nature to look at things that way, always trying to figure out how to improve them. I know I'm a perfectionist and some people think I'm too hard on them because of it, but, first of all, I'm not as hard on anyone else as I am on myself, and second of all I think my perfectionism is one of my best assets. It means that I always think really hard about what the right thing to do is, and I try to make decisions that will benefit the most people possible, no matter what project I'm working on. People know that they can trust me to make good choices. That's why they feel comfortable putting me in positions of responsibility.

The Fall Formal is student council's biggest fundraising event of the year and it's always super fun, because it's partly a serious formal dance but partly sort of ironic and relaxed, the way we do it. Like, for example, we don't call it the Homecoming Dance even though it's always scheduled to coincide with the Homecoming game, because not everybody at our school feels strongly about football and student council respects that. There are lots of kids at Vander whose main thing is math or science (we have at least two or three kids go to MIT and Caltech every year, even though we're a public school) and, not to generalize, but those kids don't necessarily love football, but they still deserve to be able to come to their school dance and not feel excluded. So that's why we don't emphasize the football thing too much. And the whole king and queen thing, too, is a little bit ironic—like a lot of times a non-traditional kid will get crowned along with a more typical king or queen. For example, last year's Formal Queen was Isabelle Howland, who is a very gorgeous and also very friendly and down-to-earth cheerleader, but Formal King was Ralphie Lorris, who is short and chubby and, to be honest, a little Asperger's-y—he has this obsession with public transit and is always talking loudly about local bus schedules. Everybody thinks Ralphie is super funny—he's sort of like an unofficial school mascot—and when they called his name to come up to the stage and be crowned next to Isabelle, everyone clapped and cheered extra hard.

Anyway, that's the kind of dance it is, not totally serious but still basically a pretty normal event, so I was positive Jesse Halberstam would not be there, since normal events are not exactly her cup of tea. We had just started spending private time together then, we were just starting to get to know each other one-on-one, and I guess she came to the dance specifically to find me. I was there in my capacity as student council secretary, making sure things went smoothly at the ticket-taking table and also supervising the refreshment displays, and Michael was my date, of course, and he was helping me reorganize the soft drinks according to flavor and sugar content when I saw Jesse come in on the other side of the gym. She was so . . . I don't know, she was a hundred percent strange looking like always, "dressed up" in this totally bizarre powder-blue man's pantsuit with a ruffled silk tuxedo shirt and bell-bottoms over those boots—those hideous rubber boots! *With* the powder-blue polyester tuxedo! And she had sort of spiked up her blonde hair so it was kind of punk looking and crazy. I still don't know where she got her hands on that outfit; I never saw her wear it again. I watched her pay for her ticket and then she was looking around for me, scanning the crowd, and when she found me she gave me this super-intense look, like, *You. Me. Here. Now.* My stomach did a little backflip inside me. And then she disappeared into the girls' locker room annex off the side of the gym.

I knew she wanted me to follow her. I also knew that I was there with Michael and it would be impolite to leave him alone with the soft drinks, and I *also* knew that I was responsible for keeping some important logistical things going on the dance floor. But to be honest, at that point I was getting pretty annoyed with some of the people working under me on the refreshments committee (like Lauren Weiss and Kim Watson and Kimmie Hersh, to name three) because they kept putting out more and more Costco-brand cheese curls, which were the only refreshments we were serving that night, even though I told them repeatedly that they had to ration the snacks so they would last for the entire event, and all of a sudden I was just like, you know what, screw this, let them put out however many cheese curls they want, whenever they want to. And I told Michael I had to use the restroom and I went to find Jesse.

That was the first time I ever let the two parts of my life come so close together. So close they almost touched.

I hardly even remember what happened in the locker room, except that she got me over in the little laundry cubicle in the back corner and somehow I ended up sitting on top of the dryer and she was standing in front of me and she had her hands up the skirt of my dress. I remember it was hot and dark, and Jesse felt like a smooth animal; her shirt was like a second silk skin over the hot, smooth skin of her arms and shoulders. She kissed and kissed my neck and shoulders and up just behind my ears—no one had ever kissed my neck before that night—and I thought I was going to pass out. I could hardly see. It smelled like dryer sheets and hair gel in there.

I knew I couldn't be gone for too long so I made her leave after just a little bit, and when I came back into the gym and everyone was still there, dancing and laughing and drinking soft drinks and eating cheese curls, and no one knew where I had been or what I had been doing and no one even thought to *ask*, I felt this amazing new feeling come over me: not like I was all-powerful exactly, but *sort* of like I was all-powerful, like I was a little bit larger than life. For the first time, I saw that I could be in two places at once, like a superhero. At that moment in the gym, I felt like I could do anything I wanted and be anything I wanted and have everything I wanted to have in the world. And I looked around at the crappy Costco-brand snacks, and skinny sophomore Mark Salfrezi pretending to be a real DJ with his mom's sunglasses and his iPod plugged into a pair of AV speakers, and the childish harvest-themed decorations (leaves cut out of construction paper—cute, but *please*), and I just thought, this whole event could be so much better. All of it. Everything. It could all be so much more polished and classy. All we would need would be a couple of corporate sponsors, like the ones my mom gets every year for her Struggle Against Alzheimer's Gala at the Hyatt Regency ballroom in Stonington.

That was the moment I first had the idea for corporate

sponsors. I sat on it all year long, then this past summer when we were at the lake house I drafted a letter to send out to selected members of our local business community. If you want to appeal to a business, you have to think like a business. What does a business want? To make money. How do they make money? By getting more customers. And how do they get more customers? Two ways: Either 1) by making a better product, or 2) by making themselves look good to potential customers. And what could make a business look better to potential customers than showing that they support kids, who are our future? I made all this clear in the letter. I also said that in these troubled times, when public school budgets are getting slashed left and right, it's harder and harder for schools to get the basic educational resources they desperately need, and Vander has some really interesting, smart, diverse students who will certainly have important roles in shaping the world of tomorrow, and don't these businesses want to be part of all that by donating funds or services to our Fall Formal, where we raise money to improve the educational resources of the school, such as computers? (Actually, the money we raise at the Fall Formal goes to fund the senior class trip every year, but I feel like that still counts as an educational resource—last year the seniors went to Cape Cod but they stopped by Plimoth Plantation on the way, and this year they're going to Disney World, and Epcot is a very educational destination.)

I sent the final draft of the letter out two weeks ago and I've already gotten three positive responses. Betty Horn from Horn of Plenty Bakery said she would donate five hundred Death by Chocolate Brownie Bites on presentation platters (sayonara, Costco-brand cheese curls!). Laurie Meloni from Buns of Steel Boot Camp and Cross-Training Gym said she would donate a sampler of Krav Maga and mixed martial arts classes suitable for beginners that we can raffle off at the event. And Howard Willette, director of corporate communications for a Stonington-based company called NorthStar Enterprises, said I should come in and meet with him face-to-face so we can discuss possible ways for their firm to get involved with Vander.

I mean, this is incredible. I actually flipped out for a second when I got the NorthStar email. I actually cried a little. I've never been to a professional corporate meeting before, and I'm so excited to go in person to the offices of NorthStar Enterprises and represent Vander and our student body and meet with someone who might actually be able to help us take things to the next level. I feel like, in all honesty, I'm exactly the right person to build this relationship.

When I think back on it now, last year's Fall Formal was really an incredible turning point for me. It was the first time I understood that I could have both Jesse and the rest of my life and one didn't have to destroy the other. It was the first time I realized that corporate sponsorship could change the whole way student council does business. And at the end of the night, as I was slow dancing the last dance before clean-up in Michael's arms, I told him I was going to run for student council president this fall, and he said he would support me and my dreams no matter what. He told me I should always shoot for the stars.

We campaigned really hard this September—I'm really proud of how hard me and Michael worked. And even though Melissa Formosa got president, and I only ended up getting vice president because Julie Dressel quit at the last minute to focus on soccer, everything worked out perfectly in the end. Vice president has turned out to be the best possible role for me. It lets me do a ton of work behind the scenes that actually has a huge impact on the school, work that I might not have time to do if I were president. This corporate sponsorship idea is just one example. Now that I've been vice president for a couple of months, I've learned that a lot of the real power in school happens behind closed doors, where the general public doesn't even see it. I've realized that I'm right where I want to be.

5

Jesse

It's so early there's still a silvery sheen of dew on the grass around Vander High. The Saturday morning sun is a puddle in the dingy sky, and Jesse stands in its watery light watching her mother's car recede down the access road away from school. She has five bucks, her phone, her notebook, a pen, and her Swiss Army Knife in the pockets of her cargo pants and a crumpled sack lunch in her hand. She didn't watch her mother pack it, but she's guessing it's the health-food version of death-row cuisine: five rice crackers in a used Ziploc bag, soggy bulgur-wheat salad in a curry-stained Tupperware container, two leathery dried apricots in a paper towel, as appetizing as a pair of shriveled human ears. "Enjoy," her mother said to her grimly as she handed it to her through the passenger's-side window. "Call me if they violate your human rights. I'll see you at five."

It's weird to be at school on a Saturday. Empty of inhabitants, it feels creepy somehow, like an abandoned factory, a ghost town. The reflective windows look dead to Jesse, concealing nothing behind them but desks, blackboards, and silence.

Jesse sits down on the damp wooden bench under the crab-apple tree by the side door. She's supposed to meet the ASP supervisor there *"promptly at 8:00 a.m.,"* the disciplinary ticket reads in Snediker's unnervingly tiny, square-cornered handwriting. The bench is deeply grooved with gouged-out graffiti—LOVE YOU MATT—SK8 OR DON'T—JIZBIZ WAZ HERE—SENIORS 4EVA—and Jesse fingers the smooth bullet of the Swiss Army Knife in her pocket, imagining for a moment what it would feel like to carve JH LOVES EM into the bench. She closes her hand around the knife, then feels a hot flush of embarrassment even thinking about doing such a thing. She pulls her hand out of her pocket, wiggles her toes around vigorously inside her boots to distract herself from the thought of Emily.

A car turns onto the access road and wends its way toward Jesse, a beat-up pea-green hatchback, crazy with hippie bumper stickers, traveling in a cloud of bouncy music that gets louder and clearer the closer it comes. It accelerates to a squealing stop in front of Jesse's bench and the passenger's-side window rolls down jerkily.

"Halberstam?" a small, bearded, long-haired elf in a

black ski hat yells out cheerfully from the driver's seat. Jesse nods.

"Where's Meinz?" he yells. Jesse shrugs, not sure what this means. The music—plinkety, happy, banjo-y—is up so loud on the car stereo that even from twenty feet away Jesse can make out every word. "I will get by," the singers promise in crooned unison.

"Parking," the elf yells, and waves enthusiastically, like a little kid. Automatically, Jesse waves back, then thinks, *Why are we waving?*

The hippiemobile pulls away, heading for the side parking lot, and at the same time up the access road a figure comes loping, hunched over, hurrying. As it gets closer, Jesse can see it's a girl. She's wearing a shapeless navy-blue overcoat and a long black skirt that reaches halfway down her shins, and she's carrying a big lumpy black tote bag over one shoulder. Her dark hair is braided in two rough braids, the left one substantially thicker than the right. As she runs—almost lurches—up the hill, her canvas slip-on shoes fall half off her feet with every step. Jesse recognizes her dimly from around school, but she's never seen her up close. The girl comes to a panting stop in front of the bench, her cheeks rosy from exertion, coarse hairs flying loose from her braids, which seem somehow to be undoing themselves from their rubber bands in real time as Jesse looks at them. The girl's eyes are cool blue in her overheated face. She doesn't smile.

"ASP?"

Jesse nods.

"I'm Esther."

"Jesse."

"Is Huckle not here yet?"

"Who's Huckle?"

The girl looks around her impatiently.

"I *ran* here and Huckle's not even here yet?"

Esther blows the hair off her damp forehead, wipes the sweat off her upper lip broadly with the sleeve of her coat—somehow the gesture reminds Jesse of an old man— and sits down heavily on the bench next to Jesse, dropping her tote bag on the ground and immediately slipping her bare feet out of her black canvas shoes. The heat from her body hits Jesse in a wave. She smells sweet and clammy, like red peppers left too long in a Tupperware container.

"He'll be here," Esther assures Jesse, not looking at her. "He sometimes has time-management issues."

Esther rummages in the tote bag by her feet and pulls out a thick, battered paperback book. She brings her legs up under her so she's sitting cross-legged on the bench and tucks her skirt around them so her knees are completely covered, like a statue of the Buddha. She opens the book with her left hand and holds it right up to her face to read, chewing at the nail of her right thumb absently. As suddenly as she arrived here, she's gone—disappeared into the book that she holds five inches away from her face. Jesse can't help but stare at her.

Esther bites down hard on the skin at the corner of her thumbnail, gnaws at it, sucks blood out of it. Jesse blinks.

"Hey, miscreants," calls the elf from behind them. Jesse turns to see him waving from the corner of the school building, holding a pair of rakes with his left hand. "Let's get cracking." He grins.

"Huckle," Esther says, an explanation. "Our supervisor." She snaps her book shut and shoves it down deep into her tote bag, slips back into her shoes and heads over toward the elf, leaving Jesse behind.

"It's gravel raking again," Huckle is saying to Esther regretfully as Jesse reaches them. "Sorry."

"Fine by me," Esther replies. She turns to Jesse. "They get deliveries of these big heaps of gravel out at the edges of the athletic fields and it's our job to spread them out evenly in the ditches. To collect the rain drainage, right?" She directs the last to Huckle, who shrugs amiably.

"Do I look like I know about rain drainage or whatnot? Am I a groundskeeper of some sort?" Huckle is wearing slouchy striped Guatemalan pants under his nubbly woven poncho-hoodie. As he talks, Jesse notices that one of his front teeth is gray. "I just check y'all in and sign y'all out. All I know about gravel is that spreading it looks like *no fun*."

"It's not fun," Esther agrees, businesslike. "But it's meditative."

"You've done this before?" Jesse asks her.

"Who, Meinz?" Huckle points at Esther. "This one? This one's been here almost every week this year, haven't you, Meinz?" Esther shrugs noncommittally. "Meinz is my main ASP buddy. If Meinz doesn't come on a Saturday, I get lonely. What're you in for this week, Meinz?"

"Protesting the mandatory spirit assembly," says Esther.

"Hey, me too." Jesse smiles, but Esther gives her a puzzled look.

"Really? I didn't see you in the office."

"Oh . . ." Somehow, suddenly, Jesse knows that the real story of her spirit assembly "protest" will not impress this girl. "I was, um, somewhere else," she fumbles.

"Spirit assembly?" Huckle laughs. "Now you're even protesting spirit assemblies? What do you have against spirit assemblies, Meinz?"

"Spirit assembly supports football. Football is a war simulation. I don't support war in any form, real or simulated."

"Hard-core," Huckle says to Jesse, jerking his thumb in Esther's direction. Jesse nods. Esther thumps her tote bag down on the wet ground and bends to rummage in it.

"Yeah, so, as far as instructions go for today, you got your rakes, you got your gravel, you got your ditches, you get the picture. I'll hold on to your bags and your phones for, you know, safekeeping, and you come get me in the phys. ed. office at noon for lunch. If I'm not there, you know, check my car. Sometimes I'm in my car during certain periods of the day. Just chilling."

Huckle smiles a big gray-toothed Cheshire-Cat smile.

From the tote bag, Esther produces her paperback, which she slips into the neck of her coat so that it vanishes, absorbed into the bulky mass of her clothes, and a crumpled-up floppy pink sunhat, which she shakes out to its full, twenty-inch diameter and sets on her head, tying the strings in a big bow beneath her chin. Without looking at Jesse she says, "Even on a cloudy day, UV rays can cause damage. We'll be out there awhile." Then she takes one of the rakes from Huckle, deposits her tote bag at his feet, and starts off purposefully toward a distant corner of the lacrosse field.

"Implement?" Huckle says to Jesse, a note of apology in his voice, extending the second rake toward her. She trades him her phone and her backpack for the tool and heads off across the field after Esther, breaking into a jog to try to close the distance between them.

* * *

The raking isn't hard at the start. It's just boring, and loud—the harsh *skritch* of the metal rakes on the jagged pebbles bores a hole into Jesse's skull right at the back of her head.

The gravel is freshly pulverized and it smells sharp and chalky, sending up clouds of stony dust whenever Jesse digs into it with the tines of her rake.

Jesse rakes halfheartedly, distracted by watching Esther out of the corner of her eye. Esther at work is awkward and fierce, flinging the rake out and hauling it back in, flinging and hauling, over and over again. Sometimes her lips move a little as she works, as if she's reciting something to herself, or she shakes her head suddenly, briefly, as if saying no to an invisible interlocutor. Esther is so focused on her job and whatever it is that's going on inside her head that Jesse imagines she wouldn't look up once until lunchtime if Jesse didn't get her attention on purpose.

"So you hate pep rallies, too," she opens, a little louder than normal to make sure Esther hears her.

Esther pauses and looks around, confused, as if trying to identify the source of the sound she just heard.

"You hate pep rallies, too?" Jesse repeats.

Esther makes eye contact with her: *Oh, it's you talking.*

"I oppose them," she corrects, and turns back to her raking.

"Me too. I find them hideous."

"Where were you registering your objection, if not the main office?"

"I was actually . . ." Jesse begins, then pauses to consider whether she should tell Esther the truth. Esther looks up briefly and nods, a bit impatiently.

"Yes?"

"I was actually trying to skip the assembly and Snediker busted me climbing out the window of the girls' room."

For a second Esther doesn't respond, and Jesse thinks it was a mistake to admit this. But then, to Jesse's relief, Esther laughs, sudden and seal-like, a kind of bark-yelp. When Esther opens her mouth, Jesse notices that her teeth are neat, small, and separate—baby teeth in a grown-up mouth.

"Oh well," Esther says. "I guess *that* was a mistake."

"Yeah, big mistake," Jesse agrees, encouraged, "especially since I was planning to use first period to put up my new manifesto around school." Somehow it's very important to Jesse that this girl know that she's serious about things.

"Oh, that's you?" Esther raises her eyebrows, curious. "Those manifesto posters, those are you?"

"My organization." Jesse nods casually, a quiet pride spreading inside her.

"I like those."

"Thanks."

"I look forward to them." That this girl knows her manifestos, likes them, looks forward to them, sends Jesse's heart sailing. "They're hilarious. They're sort of like episodes of some sitcom about a goofy activist or something."

Jesse's heart hits the ground with a thunk.

"Sitcom?"

"Yeah, they're a parody, right? Like a joke on political manifestos?"

It seems too late, or too complicated, or just too embarrassing for Jesse to correct Esther. How could she possibly explain at this moment that the manifestos are her earnest work, her best idea about how to change the culture of the school?

"Yeah," Jesse says, trying to swing a note of bravado into her voice. "Totally. A joke on manifestos."

"That's cool. Like *The Daily Show* or something, right? Satire? That's cool." Somehow when Esther says the word *cool* it's like your grandma trying to say the word *cool*. Her moist, wide mouth makes the word come out all awkward. And yet it's also completely sincere. "I mean, that kind of comedy doesn't change the world or anything, but it's funny. It gets people's attention. And it can get people thinking."

"Yeah. I always try to get people thinking."

Esther stops raking now, holds the rake away from her body and looks at Jesse thoughtfully, sizing her up.

"What's your organization called again?"

"Um, NOLAW?"

"Which stands for . . . ?"

Jesse swallows. "National Organization to Liberate All Weirdos?"

THE DIFFERENCE BETWEEN **YOU** AND **ME**

"Right, very funny. And who are your other members?"

"Um . . ." Jesse pictures herself alone at her desk in her room, cutting and pasting, running the posters off in furtive batches on her mom's printer/scanner/copier before she gets home from work. "We don't have too many members. We're not that big an organization."

"You know what you could do," Esther offers, "is join up with *my* new organization, SPAN. Have you heard of us?" Jesse shakes her head. "SPAN? Student Peace Action Network?" Jesse shakes her head again, and Esther sighs, annoyed.

"Sorry?" Jesse offers.

"No it's okay, it's just, this is our hugest problem. We've had two meetings already, me and Ms. Filarski, our faculty advisor, and we've submitted an application to be recognized as an official student group, but still nobody knows about us."

"Yeah, I never heard of you," Jesse confirms.

"You should help us." Esther peers at Jesse directly, almost confrontationally, now. "You should bring NOLAW's poster-making operation over to SPAN. We could join forces. Then we could both, like, do a better job of getting the word out about our activities, and both of us could get more members. You guys clearly have a really good public relations operation. Margaret says half of activism is advertising. She says you have to let people know what you're doing, otherwise it won't have any impact on the world.

But that kind of stuff doesn't come naturally to me."

"Who's Margaret?"

"Oh, she's my best friend and mentor and adopted grandmother. She organizes a peace vigil with her husband, Charlie, that I go to every Sunday. You should come."

"Yeah, maybe."

"You should definitely come!" Esther practically shouts, overtaken by new enthusiasm. "It's on the common in front of the Town Hall, it's only an hour, from noon to one. Margaret and Charlie have been doing it every Sunday for forty years, they're the most incredible people you'll ever meet in your life. You have to come."

"Okay."

Jesse takes a second now to look Esther over. She's completely abandoned her raking at this point and is using the rake as a gesturing tool, waving it around as she speaks. Her eyes are flinty and fierce. She's as serious, as determined, as any kid Jesse has ever seen.

"It's hard getting people to care about important issues at this school, don't you think?"

"I guess," Jesse says. "No, totally, yeah."

"Maybe not for you since you're a comedian," Esther concedes, "but for me, I mean, I'm just a freshman, maybe I don't really know how things work here yet, but I feel like kids are so superficial here. They're not involved enough in their community. In a lot of ways I hated Sacred Heart, where I used to go, but at least people there were really into service. Everybody had a cause. Here, people are more interested in things like dances and pep rallies, it seems like."

"Yeah," Jesse agrees. "It's hard to be an outsider here."

"But no, I'm not complaining." Esther shakes her head. "It's a really good challenge for me. I feel like I was meant to come here and bring some of that spirit of service to Vander. I believe that no matter how much it might seem like people don't care, if you show them how they're connected to the things that are wrong with the world, they totally change their behavior. Don't you think?"

Jesse squints, thoughtful. "I don't know." She thinks about Emily's blank stare in the bathroom. She thinks about Wyatt: *The masses want to stay ignorant.* "I hope so," Jesse says.

"Oh no, I'm sure of it. I have a lot of faith in people. That's the whole reason I founded SPAN. SPAN is going to show people the truth about injustice in the world and get people fired up to take action. As soon as we get some members. You have to come to our next meeting." It's an assertion, not an offer. "We meet Tuesdays at three thirty in Ms. Filarski's room."

"Oh, Tuesday at three thirty I actually, sort of, already have plans." Tuesday at 3:30 Jesse has plans to be working her hands up Emily Miller's shirt in the third-floor handicapped restroom of the Samuel Ezra Minot Public Library.

"That's too bad," Esther says seriously. "We could use a few committed revolutionaries."

All her life Jesse has been writing protest letters, going with her parents to marches and demos, giving part of her allowance to PETA, participating in boycotts, and writing manifestos, and she never, ever would have called herself a "revolutionary." Here, Esther says it so casually, like you'd say, "We could use a few sophomores."

"Next Tuesday, then." Esther nods, and turns back to raking. "So how long have you been running NOLAW?"

"Um, I guess I started making the manifestos in the middle of last year? Wyatt, my best friend Wyatt, says they're a symptom of the anger issues I had about my mom being sick, but he doesn't know anything. He's a libertarian."

"Your mom was sick?"

"Oh yeah. She had cancer." Jesse tosses this out casually.

At the word *cancer* Esther's whole face alters, subtly but totally. "Oh," Esther says. "What kind?"

"Breast cancer. Pink ribbon, you know, blah blah blah."

"My mom, too," says Esther.

"Really?" Jesse's eyes widen.

"Yeah. Breast cancer."

"That's so *cool*!" Jesse blurts out, then corrects herself, stumbling over her words. "No, I mean, not *cool*, it's not cool your mom had cancer, I just mean, I never met anyone else whose mom had it, too. That's, like, so amazing." Jesse smiles.

"Yeah. My mom died a year and a half ago," Esther says.

In the quiet that follows, Jesse hears the sound of the birds in the trees around them. She feels like she never noticed before how specific their songs are. One three-note melody comes from the trees to her right, over and over again, like wind chimes, and a totally different two-note melody comes from the trees to her left. She wonders if the two birds are speaking to each other.

"Did I just freak you out?" Esther asks finally.

"No, no way." Jesse can't quite look at Esther anymore. "I'm sorry about your mom."

"It's okay," Esther says. "I'm fine. Don't be freaked out, all right?"

"I'm not. I'm not."

"Good." Esther smiles a little, encouragingly. "Let's get back to work. Huckle will let us go early if we get all three piles spread out by noon."

* * *

At lunchtime, Huckle spreads out a ratty blanket on the grass by his car, right at the edge of the parking lot, for all three of them to sit on.

"This is perfect," he says, lying back on the blanket

(59)

and putting his sandaled feet up on the bumper of his hip-piemobile. "We're still on school grounds, but we're close enough to home that I can get us sodas from the fridge if we want them."

"Huckle lives right there," Esther explains, gesturing with her chin to a little white house through the spindly woods at the parking lot's edge. She takes a bite of a peanut butter and jelly sandwich that looks like it was made in a bomb shelter during an air raid—it's torn and smeared, a total mess.

"So um, why did you drive your car here?" Jesse asks.

Huckle smiles dreamily. "I like to bring my private space with me wherever I go," he says. "In case I have an urgent need to chill at any time."

"Not to be rude or anything," Jesse says, "but you seem like sort of a weird guy to be an ASP supervisor."

"I'm unusual, yes." Huckle tears a piece of Slim Jim off with his teeth and chews it roundly.

"So, like, um, how did you get this job?"

"I used to be a sub?" Huckle turns to look at Jesse from his vantage point on the ground. "At school? And then, there was, like, an incident, and I had to stop subbing? But they were like, it's cool, we can find a place for you, and they found me this."

"Uh-hunh. What kind of—" Jesse is about to ask what kind of incident Huckle was involved in, but he interrupts.

THE DIFFERENCE BETWEEN **YOU** AND **ME**

"I used to go to this school, you know," Huckle says. "Not a very long time ago. A while ago. Kind of a really long time ago."

"Yeah? Did you like it?"

"I loved it, man, I have to confess. But things are to-tally different now. You have Snediker? Snediker send you here?"

"Of course."

"That is one sad, sad lady. That lady is *compromised,* man. She used to be the world's raddest social studies teacher, back in the olden days. She had us do, like, role-playing games? And watch movies about, like, Che Guevara? And then something happened to her, man, I don't know. She changed. And now the whole school is different since they put her in charge."

"Don't you hate working for her, then?" Jesse asks. She tries to imagine slouchy Huckle, with his loose pants and stringy hair, taking orders from clenched little Snediker, and can't make the picture come together in her mind.

"Yeah, but I gotta eat, man," Huckle says philosophically. "Gotta pay rent. The freakin' Foot Locker fired me, the freakin' Whole Foods fired me 'cause of that thing with the pie. I have a small problem with supervisors, I guess. And with this job, it's weekends only, I get to be on my own a lot, I get to be outdoors. And spend time in my car."

"Jesse's going to come with me to the vigil on Sunday,"

Esther tells Huckle. To Jesse she says, "I've been trying to get Huckle to come to the vigil for weeks, but he won't do it."

"I love peace, man, but I don't need to stand around on a street corner waiting for it to come."

Huckle smiles lazily and closes his eyes.

Esther leans over to Jesse. "Don't worry," she says. "It's not just standing around. You'll see on Sunday. It's amazing."

Esther

My first hero: Joan of Arc.

Before I could even read, I had a picture book about her. My mother got it for me, and she used to read it to me all the time before she got sick. Then I read it to myself basically every day from fourth grade through sixth grade. I was obsessed with Joan. More than anything in the world I wanted to meet her. Or follow her. Or be her.

In the first couple of pages of the book, they set the scene: France, early 1400s. The country is occupied by the English, who rape and pillage and terrorize the country-side every few weeks to make sure the French peasants don't get any ideas about rising up and fighting for their freedom. Everybody hates the English, but nobody knows what to do about them: the true king, King Charles VII, is weak and pitiful, not powerful enough to oppose the English and assume the throne of his own country.

The French peasants are exhausted. They're sick.

They're suffering. They have long since stopped expecting their lives to get better.

Then one day, in a field about a mile from the tiny village of Domrémy, sitting on a stone wall watching her father's flock, a thirteen-year-old girl named Joan hears a sound. It's a voice—she can tell it's a voice because it's saying her name—but it's not human. It's not like any voice she's ever heard on this earth. It's huge and silvery and multiple—really three voices braided into one—and it seems to come from the entire sky, falling all around her like mist, like rain. It's her angels, come to give her instructions from God.

"Get up," the angels tell Joan. "Find your way to the town of Vaucouleurs. Cut your hair off and dress like a boy—people will take you more seriously that way. Get a rich man to help you secure an audience with exiled King Charles. Tell him you are come to lead an army on his behalf and drive the hated English out of France and restore him to his rightful throne. Lead an army of ten thousand men into battle. Slay the oppressors. Liberate your country. On your mark, get set—go."

Naturally, she's petrified. She argues with them, as all prophets argue with their voices at first. "This is crazy," she tells the messengers from God. "I can't be the One. I'm illiterate. I'm a teenager. I'm a girl."

"Sorry," say the angels. "God says it's you."

It takes a couple of years for the angels to convince her,

but eventually, Joan does it. She runs away from her family and prepares in secret. In the best picture in the book they show Joan sitting in a narrow stone room, peering at herself in a small, spotted medieval mirror. She's holding up a long hank of hair, getting ready to shear it off with a knife. The other half of her head is already cut short. She looks like a half boy, half girl in the picture, but the look she's giving herself in the mirror isn't confused—it's determined.

She does all of it, everything the angels told her to do. She finds the rich guy, gets him to take her to the true king, convinces the king to let her lead his army, gets a suit of armor and a horse and an embroidered heraldic banner, leads ten thousand men into battle, plans surprise attacks, liberates the besieged city of Orléans. Overnight she becomes famous in France and infamous in England. The French call her the Maid, the Lark, and the Messenger. The English call her witch, cow, sorceress, and whore.

Secretly, I believed I was the new Joan. I could feel it inside me, my destiny—not to lead an army, maybe, but to do something big that would save the world. I was positive that before my twelfth birthday I would hear my own voices and get my own holy instructions. I tried to put myself into places where they would feel comfortable coming to me—gardens, athletic fields, big outdoor spaces. I waited to be told what God had planned for me to do.

Twice I was Joan for Halloween, in fourth and fifth

grade. My mother wouldn't let me cut off my hair, but she did make me a helmet out of a gallon milk jug turned upside-down and spray-painted silver, and she helped me tuck my braids up inside it.

By the time I was thirteen, I realized they weren't coming for me. I never heard anything directly from God, and I ended up not being able to be outside as much because my mother got sick and I had to be inside all the time, in hospital rooms, in hospital hallways, in waiting rooms, in parking garages, in diners, drinking Coke with lemon while my dad drank coffee and looked out the window.

In the end, she was burned. Joan. In the end she did everything a human being could do, everything her voices told her to do, and still the English captured her, tortured her, starved her, shaved her head, put her through a five-month show trial, and finally burned her at the stake in a public square. She died forgiving her executioners through the flames.

In the end, my mother chose to come home. She had been through years of treatments that felt more like punishments than cures—radiation and chemicals and surgeries and poisons—and she said she couldn't bear to die of something that was supposed to heal her. She wanted to die comfortable and calm, in our house, with us. She wanted to let her body stop naturally. My father thought this was a terrible idea, and he was really badly behaved about it. He said a lot of cruel things to her that I'll never forget. He told her she was selfish, which was especially unfair. But my mother could be incredibly stubborn when she believed she was right. In the end, she got what she wanted. She was home for thirty days. She died in the temporary hospital bed we set up for her in the living room. Two days before she died, she told my father she forgave him for all the awful things he'd said.

My father couldn't handle speaking at the funeral so I did it for him. I wrote a eulogy for her, describing the interesting, kind person she was and listing all the things I loved about her. I talked about the main things she liked to do: gardening, doing hair, reading, volunteering at church. I talked about her sweet voice, her soft hands, and how incredibly stubborn she could be when she believed she was right.

In the end, France was occupied until 1453, another twenty-two years after Joan was executed. But in 1920, they made her a saint.

7

Jesse

"It was all fine until right before the end," Wyatt recounts as he tails Jesse, a brisk step and a half behind her, through the sunny autumn afternoon. Somewhere in the stacks of the Samuel Ezra Minot Public Library, two blocks away, Emily Miller is getting ready to go on break. When Jesse meets up with her at 3:30—ten minutes from now—in the third-floor handicapped restroom, it will be the first time they've seen each other since the Spirit Assembly Bathroom Incident, and Jesse has been working on some choice words she wants to say. Jesse picks up the pace a little and lengthens her stride, and Wyatt skips to keep up with her. She has already told him twice—though he's pretended not to hear—that she can't actually hang out today.

"We were chatting like perfect ladies, very civilized," Wyatt continues. "I was lulled into a sense of false security.

He hardly even asked me anything about myself, he didn't make one snide comment about the homeschooling, he didn't ask me whether my mother was taking her meds, he just went on and on telling me this insanely dull story about Stepmama Louise and her epic battles with the bunny rabbits who live in their backyard and eat her flowers—apparently, she started out poisoning them with rat bait, but now she's using, like, a blowtorch on them, shooting them with flames off the side of the deck. And I was all, 'Ha-ha, that Louise is a real spitfire, ha-ha, what a great assassin of bunny rabbits Louise is,' and then he paid and we left the café, and I was like, oh my God, he's not even going to mention it, I'm home free, this is the dawning of a new era. And then right when we got to the car he was like, 'So, did you get the literature I sent you?'"

"Oh no, the ex-gay pamphlets?"

"The ones I shredded."

"What did you say?"

"I told him they were too pornographic for me so I threw them out."

"You told him they were *pornographic*?" Jesse wails.

"They have a half-naked man on the cover! He's hanging up there on that cross all muscular and cut with nothing but a little gym towel on—it's pornographic!"

"He must have gone ballistic."

"Worse, he was totally calm. He said, 'Son, I'm asking

you to please reckon with your choices. I don't want you to spend eternity paying for your sins in hell.' I said to him, 'Howard, thank you so much for the advice, but I'll take my chances.'"

"The point of these dates is to be *nice* to him so he'll still pay for college, not to antagonize him and make him want to disown you forever."

"I know, but I couldn't help myself, he's such an irrational idiot. And my comic sidekick wasn't there to support me."

"I'm sorry," Jesse repeats. "I'm sorry, I'm sorry. I'll be there next time, I swear."

"Saturday the thirtieth, okay? Ten thirty a.m." Wyatt steps in front of Jesse and puts his hands on her shoulders so he can stare deeply into her eyes. His dark, tendrilly curls are wild around his pale face. In his red-and-white-checked thrift-store Western shirt with the silver-buttoned pockets and the pointy collar embroidered with red, bucking horses, he looks a tiny bit like a chorus girl from *Annie Get Your Gun*. "Please be there. I don't like to beg, but please, please, please."

"Saturday the thirtieth, ten thirty. I will be there."

"You'll have to behave yourself in school. No more alternative suspensions. Can you keep your antisocial tendencies in check long enough to avoid Snediker for that one week?"

"Absolutely. I promise."

Jesse breaks Wyatt's gaze briefly to check her watch—3:24. T minus six minutes till Emily.

"Late for something?" Wyatt asks, mildly suspicious. No gesture of Jesse's, not even the most discreet watch-check, escapes Wyatt's attention.

"No, I just, I really have to get started on this homework. I'm sorry but I told you, I can't actually hang out today."

"Yes, I actually heard you the first six times you said that, and I have to work, too," says Wyatt, just a bit testily. "I won't bug you."

"What are you working on, a historically accurate diorama of Ayn Rand's first apartment?"

"Actually . . ." Wyatt lets his gaze drift vaguely up to the air above Jesse's head. "I'm applying to do study abroad next semester, and I have to write an essay for it."

Jesse stops walking.

"What do you mean, study abroad? Study abroad where?"

"I don't know. Denmark, maybe. Somewhere where the boys are tall and dreamy."

They've reached the library and Wyatt starts to head up the sidewalk to the front door, but Jesse grabs his arm to stop him.

"Excuse me, but what are you talking about? I mean, what are you *talking* about, Denmark? You can't go to Denmark next semester, that's ridiculous."

"It's not ridiculous, it's intercultural exchange. The American Field Service runs it. My mom thought it might be a good thing for me." Wyatt's trying to sound breezy, but he just sounds guilty and strained. He hasn't made eye contact with Jesse since he dropped this bomb—he keeps looking over her head or just past her shoulder.

"But Denmark is, like, practically a socialist country! You'd hate it there!"

Despite the distance that has grown up between them, Jesse still can't imagine making it through sophomore year without talking to Wyatt every night and seeing him at least a couple of times a week.

"Just because they have the wrong idea about how to run their government doesn't mean I can't enjoy their fjords and clean public transit and herring-based cuisine," Wyatt says. "If they even have fjords. I believe they have fjords. Anyway, I probably won't even get accepted. I have to write an essay for the application about what I personally am willing to do to promote equality between nations. Obviously, my real opinions on that topic are unlikely to impress anyone at the American Field Service. As you know, I believe that all countries are equal, but some countries are more equal than others. I may have to lie about my beliefs."

Wyatt chunks open the heavy library door, and Jesse follows him inside.

The Minot Public Library is one of the places Jesse

knows best in the world. Before they renovated it, it was just like a big, old, funky Victorian house overflowing with books from floor to ceiling, with worn, blood-red Oriental carpets on the floors and mismatched chairs and tables set out here and there for patrons to sit at. There were so many books that some of them were just laid out in stacks on side tables, or shelved in weird cabinets like where you'd keep dishes in your dining room. Some of the categories were strange, too—traces of the curious mind of some long-lost librarian who ignored the Library of Congress and organized the place according to her own interests and predilections: Cowboy Romances, Science FACTion, Travel Guides for the Elderly and Infirm, Intergalactic Adventure Stories. If you wanted to find anything, you had to already know where it was.

Growing up, Jesse knew every corner of every room. She knew exactly where to find her favorite picture books in the children's room, and she even had favorite toys she would visit on a regular basis. The stuffed animals were overloved and overhandled—communally owned by every kid in town—and they smelled like mold and sand when she brought them up to her face to kiss them, but she adored them anyway: the long, rainbow-striped worm; the thin-furred, floppy-necked dog. As a kid, every time she walked in the front door she would rub the belly of the statue of the bronze boy holding his fishing rod on his shoulder that stood in the corner of the foyer next to the creaky stairs. It was a ritual; it didn't feel right to pass him without greeting him that way. For a long time he was taller than she was. Then she was taller than he was. Then one day she read the little bronze plaque on the base by his bare feet and realized that he wasn't just some random country boy going fishing, he was supposed to be Huck Finn, from the books by Mark Twain. Somehow after that she didn't feel close to him anymore, and she never rubbed his belly again.

A couple of years ago, the library had a massive fund drive and raised the money to tear off the back half of the building and add on a big, bright new addition—three stories of stacks, a new community room in the basement, an airy atrium for the periodicals section with couches and armchairs for people to sit and read the newspaper in. It's nice and everything, and much tidier and easier to find things in than the old building, but Jesse feels like the renovation kind of killed the library. The gloomy, odd-shaped rooms, the toffee-dark wood of the old banister, the secret place to hide under the stairs that were the best parts of the library's back half have all been replaced by an impersonal, featureless newness. The new part of the building feels like a chain hotel. She never goes back there unless she absolutely has to.

But this is where Wyatt leads her today. He loves the big communal reading table in the periodicals room, right

in the center of the new atrium. Jesse hates to sit here—
it feels so public, so glaringly bright—but Wyatt is determined. He's not even finished unpacking his stuff to work
when she jumps up from the seat beside him.

"I have to go to the bathroom," she whispers apologetically. "I'll be right back. Save my seat."

Jesse bounds up the back stairs two at a time and
emerges into the dark of the third floor. The upstairs of the
Minot is untouched by the renovation, and the big third-
floor room still houses the old Mystery and True Crime
section, the Local Revolutionary War History section, and
the Cookbook Memoir section. Around a corner and down
a long, narrow hall lined with dormer windows is the upstairs handicapped restroom. It's the dumbest place in the
world for a handicapped restroom (up a flight of stairs?
down a narrow hall?), which is maybe why no one ever
goes in there. And why it's the perfect place for Jesse and
Emily's weekly meetings.

Emily works as a circulation assistant, shelving books,
after school on Tuesday afternoons. She's the one who
found this place for them, and she's already in there today,
waiting impatiently, when Jesse knocks the secret knock
(*knock knock*, pause, *knock knock*, pause, *knock*). Emily
opens the door a crack, grasps Jesse's hand, and pulls her
inside.

"You're late," she says before Jesse can even say hello.

"I only have a few minutes left on my break, and I've been *dying* to see you. I've been waiting all week for you to walk in that door."

Jesse has planned to say, *We have to talk about what happened on Friday.* She has planned to say, *From now on, I don't want to pretend we don't know each other when we see each other in public.* She has planned to say, *I don't know how much longer I can do this.* But Emily pulls Jesse close, slips her arms around her neck, and presses her sweet, soft mouth against Jesse's.

Jesse dissolves.

Kissing Emily is literally the best thing Jesse has ever done. In her life. There is no feeling more right or more perfect than the feeling of having Emily in her arms. It makes Jesse feel larger than life—superpowerful—to touch this girl and be touched by her.

Every time they kiss, no matter how into it Emily seems, she always starts out a little tense, a little jumpy, and it's Jesse's job to soothe her, coax her closer, seduce her into the deep making out. Jesse holds her tightly and kisses her gently, and at a certain point, every time, she feels the little latch holding Emily together give way. Then Emily's head falls back, her neck loosens, her shoulders drop, her fingers relax—she comes a little bit undone in Jesse's arms. Jesse gathers her up and pushes her back against a handy wall (or tree, or window, or car door— but usually wall, almost always a bathroom wall) and feels

Emily open up to her, draw her in with her entire body.

Emily's face, so sunny-cheerful in everyday life, so bright and cute and alert, deepens and darkens when Jesse is kissing her. Her eyes fill with smoke and fall half closed, her cheeks flush. Sometimes she slurs her words. A lazy, wicked expression comes over her face, like she's a little bit hungry and a little bit dangerous—good for nothing, ready to do damage. She can stop Jesse's heart when she looks at her like this.

When Jesse is kissing Emily, it is all she wants to do for as long as she lives. The kissing becomes her first and last name, her only skill, the reason she was born and the way she wants to die. Most of the time while they're kissing, it's impossible for her to imagine how she even made this happen in the first place. How can she have gotten this girl—*Emily Miller!*—to kiss her at *all*, let alone to *keep* kissing her, to come and meet her in secret every *week* to kiss her? It's a miracle. It's the best thing that has ever happened. While it's happening.

"I have five minutes," Emily breathes, and Jesse slips two fingers into Emily's ponytail holder and tugs it off, Emily pulling free from it and then shaking out her thick, caramel hair so Jesse can wind her fingers through it. Emily's hair smells like coconut and pears; Jesse hugs her close and buries her face in the hair at the back of her neck, breathes in the smell deeply. While she's there she kisses Emily's hairline, then moves her lips down along the warm ridge of her shoulder, then along the satin curve of her collarbone in the front. Emily exhales and drops her head back, giving Jesse room. Jesse reaches up with her left hand and undoes the top button of Emily's sweater, then the second button. (It's the pink J.Crew cardigan with the fake pearl buttons.) She folds the neck of the sweater back and exposes the line of Emily's white cotton bra, kisses down along the swell of the top of her breast, the delicate skin there as light and sweet as meringue against Jesse's tongue as she kisses lower and closer.

Emily breathes, then breathes deeper. Her breath catches in her throat as Jesse kisses into the V at the center of her bra, then slips her whole hand up over Emily's right breast. Emily leans into Jesse's palm and whispers, "Yes." Jesse pushes Emily back against the wall and looks up at her face; it is a picture of total surrender, her eyes closed, her mouth open, her chin tipped up so her long, pale neck is exposed. In a burst of desire, Jesse peels Emily's bra back to expose her naked breast. Emily pulls back abruptly and stands up straight, shaking her head.

They have some rules that they haven't ever said out loud to each other but that they both always follow. Jesse just broke one.

"I'm sorry," Emily says, pulling her sweater closed at the neck. She seems flustered, but mostly genuinely apologetic. "I want to. I wish I could, but I can't."

"I know," Jesse mumbles, furiously embarrassed. "I shouldn't have. I'm sorry."

"No, no, it's okay." Emily turns away from Jesse to re-button her sweater.

"It was dumb. It was stupid."

"No, no, it's okay. I have to go back to work anyway."

Emily bends at the waist sharply, flipping her tousled hair forward, then whips back up into a standing position so her hair fans out straight and neat down her back. Jesse looks down at her rubber boots dully, at the dingy, tessellated tiles on the floor beneath them.

"I'm so glad I got to see you, even for a second," Emily says pleasantly, in a voice a bank teller might use with a well-liked regular customer. She turns back toward Jesse as she regathers her hair into a ponytail—the same ponytail Jesse disassembled just moments ago. She looks past Jesse at her own reflection in the mirror as she twists her perfumed mane up into a single cable, swift and sure, snaps it through its stretchy tie and tightens it up.

"I kind of, actually, wanted to talk to you about something," Jesse says, low, halting.

"Yeah?" Emily smiles. "About what? I only have a few seconds, so . . . but what?"

She gives Jesse a look that exactly matches the one she gave her in the girls' room on Friday morning—brightly lit emptiness, like a sunny, unfurnished room. In a flash,

Jesse pictures herself reaching for Emily in a dozen different bathrooms, a hundred different closets, a thousand different hidden secret stairwells forever. . . .

"I . . ."

"Yeah?" Emily's expression doesn't change, doesn't expand or contract even a fraction of an inch.

"I feel like, I don't know, I feel like . . ."

Now Emily tips her head to the side and scrunches up her eyes and nose into her pity face.

"I *so* want to talk to you about whatever you want to talk to me about?" she promises, hyper-sincere. "But I'm already late coming off break, I have to go back and clock in with Carol. Is it, like, something that can wait for next time? Or maybe you can email me about it?"

"I feel like we can't do this anymore," Jesse blurts out, and as soon as she's said it she feels both relieved and crushed with sadness.

A ripple of something passes through Emily's face, something strong and violent that Jesse can't quite identify—panic? terror? rage?—and then it's gone, dissolved into the shimmering sunshine of her perpetual smile.

"Okay, that's crazy," Emily says firmly but lightly. "I know it's hard right now, but it's fine, we're fine."

"I'm not." Jesse feels like she's talking like a caveman—grunts and monosyllables. It's so hard to get out complete sentences when she's talking to Emily Miller. What she really wants to say is, *It's not hard right now, it's always been hard, and it's never going to get any easier. You're going to go to this year's Fall Formal with Mike McDade instead of me, and you're going to go to next year's Fall Formal with Mike McDade instead of me, and you're going to go to college with Mike McDade and get married to Mike McDade and have babies with Mike McDade instead of me, and I'm sorry but I'm not fine about it!*

"You are *totally* fine." Emily gives her reflection a brisk, final once-over in the mirror, then steps up to Jesse and takes hold of her by the shoulders. "Listen," she says seriously, looking deep into Jesse's eyes and reaching up to stroke her jawline with two fingers. "I know this isn't perfect, I know it's super complicated, but it's the best we can do now, right? And I actually think it's pretty good. We have a really good time together, don't we?"

Jesse just nods.

"We have an incredible time together, because we're incredible together. We have something incredible between us, you and me."

Jesse nods again.

"I mean, it sucks not to see each other more, I miss you all the time and I'm always wishing I could be with you more, but when we *do* see each other, it's totally amazing, right?"

Nod.

"Because *you're* amazing. You're not like anyone else I've ever known. You're not like anyone else in the world."

Jesse rolls her eyes but she can feel herself blushing. The skin where Emily is stroking her tingles under her feathery touch.

"I know I'm really busy and that makes it hard for us to find time to be alone together, but I have to say, I'm not even that upset about it right now, because I have a really good feeling about this fall. I feel like everything is going to work itself out. Really exciting new things are happening, and I just know that everything's going to change this year."

"Really?" Jesse can't help herself. She knows she shouldn't hear this as Emily saying *I'll be with you for real by the end of this year.* She shouldn't hear her saying *I swear I'm going to break up with Mike and make you my girlfriend and take you to prom in the spring.* Of course that's crazy. Of course that's not what she means. But somewhere in the secret inner fibers of what she's saying, Jesse feels like maybe . . . that *is* what she means?

"Totally." Emily beams. "I can feel it. This is going to be a big year for everyone. It's going to be a huge year for Vander. Everything's going to be different by the time this year's over."

Dumb with hope, Jesse smiles, and Emily leans in and kisses her smile. As their lips touch, Jesse feels her whole midsection melt into stars.

In a second it will be over. In two seconds Emily will be saying, *Wait at least a minute before you come out after me.* In a minute Emily will be gone, and in two minutes Jesse will be trudging downstairs alone, sitting back down next to Wyatt, trying to come up with a plausible explanation for why she was gone for so long. In an hour she'll be yearning so hard for Emily and feeling so rotten about herself that she'll be swearing to never see Emily again, swearing that she's just going to stop showing up for their meetings and not even bother to explain why, just cut off all communication with Emily once and for all, to save the last tiny shreds of her pride.

But for now, in this moment, Emily is still kissing her. Her tongue is alive in Jesse's mouth, her hands are clasped behind Jesse's neck, and while it's happening, it's eternal. While it's happening, it will never end.

8

Emily

It's hard for me to tear myself away from Jesse once we start kissing. I'm not going to lie about it, I get really clingy with her sometimes. We don't get that many minutes together in a normal week, and sometimes I just wish I could call in sick to work one Tuesday and we could spend the whole afternoon in the bathroom there together. Or somewhere else, somewhere nicer. Sometimes I daydream about taking her someplace, like on a camping trip somewhere, or up to the lake house someday in the off-season when no one else is there—someplace where I can have as many hours with her as I want. To do whatever I want with her, for as long as I want to do it.

But then I also think that I'm lucky we can only see each other for short amounts of time. I feel like there are certain things that I can't do with Jesse without betraying Michael, and we don't do them ever, but I get so carried away when we're together . . . if I didn't have to tear myself away from her and go back to work after fifteen minutes or half an hour, I don't know if I could trust myself to stop. Who knows what might happen if we had, like, a whole hour or more alone. I can hardly bear to think about it.

This last time we were together I felt like she was getting sort of sad about the reality of our situation, and I really wanted to reassure her as much as I could, so much so that I almost came out and told her everything about what's been going on with me and the corporate sponsorship thing. Honestly, I don't know, but I feel like this is one of the most exciting new things ever to happen to our school, it's such an incredible opportunity for us, and it feels to me like a sign that everything's going to be okay this year. Better than okay—everything's going to be fantastic.

I was this close to telling Jesse all about the totally incredible meeting I had with Howard Willette, director of corporate communications for NorthStar Enterprises, and Martha Rinaldi, assistant director of corporate communications, on Monday afternoon. They were so amazing to me, so nice and welcoming, and so professional at the same time. They referred to me as "Ms. Miller" throughout the entire meeting. On the phone when we talked last week, Mr. Willette had suggested that I write up a brief proposal of possible ways NorthStar Enterprises could get involved with Vander, so I did, like, a whole presentation about what kinds of projects student council could use help with. I started out trying to be realistic and modest in my first draft, like I said they could maybe provide hot chocolate for the volunteers who staff the outdoor drop-off sites for our winter clothing drive in the fall, or I suggested they could pay for student-designed, screen-printed T-shirts for the senior class to strengthen class unity and spirit. But when I showed my first draft to my mom, she suggested that I really try to dream big on the page, really aim high, because this meeting was my one chance to impress this large, significant, and, to be honest, very wealthy company, and I had to make my time with them count. So I went back and revised the proposal and I just went to town imagining everything I could think of that a company like NorthStar could possibly do to support our school, academically, artistically, and athletically. The proposal ended up being nine pages; I had to put it in a plastic sleeve. I titled it "VANDER'S DREAMS" in a 24-point font on the first page, and broke all my ideas down into short-term and long-term goals with, like, subheadings and charts. It was pretty amazing by the time I was done.

At the meeting, before I handed them the presentation, I gave Mr. Willette and Ms. Rinaldi a little talk introducing them to Vander as a school. I told them about Vander's past, present, and future, and I talked about our college statistics, which are some of the best in the state, and I mentioned our several famous alumni, like best-selling author of the Soul Searchers self-help books Marcy Kirby, nationally known cancer researcher Dr. Ernest Chang, and of course, Channel 8 meteorologist Don Storme. I made sure Mr. Willette and Ms. Rinaldi understood that investing in Vander is investing in the future, not just of our town and of our state but of our country.

Then I handed them the presentation.

I hate to say it, but they *loved* me. They were so into every word I said. They went nuts over the proposal—Mr. Willette had Ms. Rinaldi run off a bunch of color copies right then while I was sitting there. By the time the meeting was over, not only had Mr. Willette agreed to underwrite the Fall Formal—everything about it! food and entertainment and supplies and roving photographer and everything! all we have to do is use their name somehow in the title of the event!—he had also agreed to partner with Vander's athletics department to improve the facilities and fields for our teams, and—this is the craziest, most amazing part—he had offered me an unpaid internship with the corporate communications department of NorthStar Enterprises. Seriously. Six to eight hours a week. He offered me a job, just based on my professional performance in this meeting.

I can safely say that this was one of the greatest afternoons of my life. And I wanted to tell Jesse about it so, so badly—it was all there, right on the tip of my tongue.

This whole thing has made me feel so hopeful about everything, and I could see that hope was what she needed to
feel right then, in the bathroom, more than anything, and
I was just dying to tell her about it.

But at the last minute I kept it general, and just talked
about my hope for the year without going into specifics
about NorthStar. We don't exactly have a great track record when it comes to talking about things from the real
world, me and Jesse. We have the most amazing connection two people could possibly have, it's almost spiritual
what's between us, but we don't really have that much in
common outside of that connection. A couple of times I've
tried to talk to her about real stuff, and each time I've tried
to explain about something I'm doing that I really care
about a lot, she's said something totally hurtful and negative to me about it. I know she's not *trying* to be hurtful
to me, she just doesn't have the broadest mind of anyone I
know, put it that way.

An example I could give is when I got involved last year
in student council's campaign to bring healthier snack
options into school to combat obesity, which is a killer.
It wasn't my idea, it was Heather Hughes's idea, because
her mom has diabetes and she has seen firsthand what
the obesity epidemic can do to a person. But as soon as
Heather proposed it in session I got on board, and I spear-
headed a proposal to the school administration to petition

Handi Snak, Inc., the company that owns and maintains the snack machines in the cafeteria, to increase the selection of snacks they offer in the machines. I did all this research about what kinds of healthier options they could be offering the students at Vander, and this one Tuesday I was trying to tell Jesse how excited I was about the whole thing, and she had barely heard like three words from me before she interrupted and was like, "Why are you letting a corporation like Handi Snak tell you what's healthy and what's not? Why don't you work with the people at the farmers' market and bring in actual fresh fruits and vegetables from local farms, which would be organic and healthy and cheap?" And in my mind I was like okay, A) that's a totally impractical idea because there's no way to store the fresh fruits and vegetables, and also in the winter there aren't any and also who's going to be in charge of preparing and selling them, and B) thanks a lot for being totally negative and dismissive about this plan I worked on for like two months to do something positive for our school. I guess, like a lot of people in our town, Jesse has a tendency to just criticize things that she thinks are wrong—she doesn't have any actual ideas or solutions for changing things she doesn't like in the world. Personally, I'm not a whiner. I don't believe in complaining about something if you don't have a realistic plan for how to fix it. Organic fruit in the vending machines at Vander is *not* a realistic solution.

Plus, that day when we got into the fight about the healthy snacks, we barely got two minutes of make-out time total, and I was just like, Okay, this is *so* not worth it. This is the last time I try to talk to her about anything from real life.

I'm sure she would have some crazy, weird objection to the NorthStar thing. I don't even know what it would be, but I can just feel that she would be like, *This violates the separation of church and state,* or whatever. And I just didn't feel like dealing with that from her right then.

That's one thing I'll say for Michael—I can talk to him about anything. If I come to him and tell him I just want him to listen to me while I work out a problem I'm having, he'll do it. He's the most perfect sounding board. I always hear girls complaining that their boyfriends don't listen to them when they talk or don't care about their lives or their feelings or their dreams, and I can't help but feel bad for them. In this way, Michael's one in a million. Most girls aren't nearly as lucky as me when it comes to their boyfriends.

When I called Michael after the NorthStar meeting, I told him all about it, every single thing, what I was wearing and what kind of fizzy water the receptionist brought me to drink while I waited and all the amazing things Mr. Willette and Ms. Rinaldi said to me during our discussion, and how productive it all was and how great for Vander. And Michael just listened supportively to me, and when I was done he told me that he admired me so much, and that he thinks it's amazing how much I care about our school. As good as I was already feeling, I felt a million times better after I got done talking to him. That's what real love does—it makes you feel like Wonder Woman, like you can achieve superhuman feats. Not everybody has real love in their life, and I know how lucky I am to have it with Michael. It's not something I would ever want to give up.

9

Jesse

When Jesse gets to the parking lot behind the Town Hall on Sunday it's ten minutes before noon, and Esther is there alone. She's bent over, facing away from Jesse, and muttering to herself as she rummages through a messy heap of cardboard signs on sticks. By her feet is her lumpy black tote bag, a thermos, two folding chairs, and what looks like a giant, rolled-up fabric scroll on two two-by-fours. Jesse recognizes this as demo equipment—it's familiar to her from years of accompanying her parents to marches, around town and in DC, for nuclear disarmament, women's rights, various wars—whatever injustice was currently lighting a fire under Fran's and Arthur's asses.

One of Jesse's earliest memories is of sitting on her father's shoulders, both arms wrapped around his balding head, looking out over a sea of people all walking in the same direction and shouting in unison. It was a march to raise awareness about the genocide in Rwanda, and Jesse was three years old. She remembers having a peace symbol painted on her cheek by a beautiful lady with long, curly hair; she remembers when the big kid wearing a NO HITTING: USE YOUR WORDS T-shirt stole her box of raisins, just swiped it right out of her hand while they were stopped at a police blockade, waiting to cross an intersection. She remembers the nasty fight her mother got into with the boy's hippie mom over the stolen raisins, remembers her father begging her mother to please stop fighting at the peace rally.

Now, watching Esther mutter and rummage by herself here in this deserted parking lot, Jesse suddenly wonders whether her description of the vigil as a fun, big-group affair was actually all in Esther's mind. What if "Margaret" and "Charlie" are actually Esther's imaginary friends, and this whole thing is some weird, loopy setup? Jesse stands, not moving, twenty feet away from Esther, and doesn't say anything. It's not too late to slip away before she's seen. Esther would never even know Jesse was here.

But suddenly, Esther lets the armful of signs drop to the ground with a clatter and stands up, muttering, "Typical, typical, *typical*!" She turns, plants her balled fists on her hips, and surveys the parking lot critically, squinting as if looking for something lost. When her eyes light on Jesse, her glowering expression resolves into a look of sweet pleasure. She smiles so big her tiny teeth show, top and bottom.

"Hey!" Esther says.

"Hey." Jesse can't help but smile back at Esther. Then she blurts out, "I thought you said there would be other people here," before she can stop herself.

Esther doesn't seem perturbed by her concern. "Oh yeah, there will be. It's only a few minutes to twelve, still—Margaret and Charlie come on Access-a-Ride so they're always here right at noon. And the rest of the group, whatever. They'll be here when they get here. A lot of them have kind of a loose relationship with time. Hold this."

Esther hoists the rolled scroll with the two-by-fours off the ground and hands it gingerly to Jesse, who takes it and bobbles it—it's way heavier than she expected.

"Careful with that, careful, careful!"

"Sorry." Awkwardly, Jesse shifts the scroll around in her arms until she has a firm grip on it.

"It's okay, it's just, that banner is an artifact. Someday they're gonna put it in the Smithsonian museum."

"What's so special about it?"

Esther gets her things together while she explains, stuffing the thermos into her already overstuffed tote, slipping her arm through the legs of the folding chairs, gathering the ungainly pile of signs up in her arms.

"Margaret and Charlie made it themselves in 1965, right at the beginning of the Vietnam War. They were some of the first people in America to protest Vietnam. It's just a couple of bedsheets they sewed together and painted, but they carried it to peace marches in, like, forty-two states over the years. They took it to Woodstock; you can see it in one part of the documentary. Did you see that Woodstock documentary?"

Jesse shakes her head. Her father had wanted to Netflix the documentary about the great rock-and-roll love-in of 1969, but her mother had insisted on putting an entire sixteen-hour miniseries of Charles Dickens' *Great Expectations* ahead of it on their queue, and somehow they hadn't made it yet from Victorian London to the Summer of Love.

"It's not that interesting a movie, but it's very cool to see Margaret and Charlie in the background in that one shot, holding this very banner. This banner has been to Hungary, Germany, France, and Japan. It's been everywhere."

"It does look kind of grungy." Jesse takes a closer look at the piece of history she's cradling. The fabric rolled around the two-by-fours is cracked and grimy, so stiff with layers of leathery gray paint it looks like dried elephant skin.

"They repair and repaint it every year," Esther explains. "And they change the lumber whenever it gets warped. Archbishop Desmond Tutu once held that banner. This way. Come on."

Esther turns and clanks toward the side of the Town Hall building, laden with tote and chairs and signs. Jesse follows.

"I'm so happy you're here," Esther calls to Jesse over her shoulder.

"Thanks." Jesse feels that same small sense of warm recognition she felt when Esther first complimented her manifestos.

"Usually, it's just me trying to haul all this stuff around myself. It's nice to have another set of hands."

"Oh." Jesse thinks to herself, *Glad I could be of service.* But she doesn't say it out loud.

When they round the corner of the Town Hall, there's already a guy waiting for them on the sidewalk about twenty yards down.

"Oh, good, Arlo's here. We set up over there, where Arlo's standing." Esther points to the waiting guy and follows her own finger in his direction.

Arlo is tall, slim, and undulant, like a giant reed in a river. He's clearly a grown-up but dressed like a kid—red Che T-shirt peeking out from under his army jacket, artlessly ripped jeans, a newsboy cap perched atop his narrow face. A sparse but silky mustache and beard ripple around his mouth and chin. He has a bundle of newspapers clamped under one arm and sips from a paper coffee cup. When he waves to Esther, his whole body seems to sway along with his hand as it arcs fluidly through the air.

"Arlo," Esther calls to him.

"Comrade," Arlo calls back.

"This is Jesse Halberstam. She's new."

"Excellent." Arlo looks briefly at Jesse with little interest, then takes a precise sip from his coffee, his lips extending toward the cup like a giraffe's.

Esther drops her armful of equipment on a patch of grass between the Town Hall and the sidewalk and begins busily but clumsily setting up for the vigil.

"Mary Catherine called," Arlo informs Esther as she struggles to open one of the folding chairs. "Paul's sick so she can't make it today. Aurora's in Burlington doing a muscular dystrophy walk, Louis has a men's group thing, and Elise is at her cousin's bar mitzvah in Keene. And Phyllis has work. So I guess it's just you, me, and Margaret and Charlie today."

"And Jesse," Esther reminds him through gritted teeth as she bears down on the stubborn folding chair, trying to force it open. It snaps into position at last with a pop, and she sighs with relief.

"And Jesse," Arlo repeats.

Esther walks ten feet down the sidewalk to plant the chair in the grass facing the street and the row of shops across it. It's the main drag of the town, and the place is humming with sunny-weekend activity; cars are driving by in a steady stream in both directions, and the stores across the street—Blue Planet Global Gifts, Beverly Coffee, Jansen's Stationery Store, Murray and Sons Hardware—are alive with people coming and going. This is a good spot, visibility-wise, for a demo, though it also occurs to Jesse now to wonder how she could have lived in this town for fifteen years and never noticed that there was a peace vigil going on in the center of town every Sunday.

"Can someone help with the other chair?" Esther calls.

Jesse looks at Arlo to see if he's going to respond to this, but he's peering into his BlackBerry now, reading something with one eyebrow arched. Jesse grabs the second folding chair—it's as light as a piece of balsa wood and opens smoothly to her touch. She holds it up with one hand.

"Where do you want it?"

Esther takes the chair and places it on the ground near where Arlo's standing. Then she turns back to the cardboard signs, arranging them faceup on the grass, fanned out so they're clearly readable. NO TO WAR. WAR IS OVER—IF YOU WANT IT. WAR IS NOT GOOD FOR CHILDREN AND OTHER LIVING THINGS. WAR: WHAT IS IT GOOD FOR? There are about ten signs, all hand-lettered in Sharpie marker on brightly colored card stock. Some are taped to rulers, some to broomsticks, some to scraps of wood. They've clearly been through some inclement weather, these signs—they're a little the worse for wear. Pretty soon, Jesse realizes, she's going to be expected to choose one to hold.

"Hang on to this end of the banner," Esther commands Jesse abruptly, pointing, "and I'll unroll it."

Jesse props one of the two-by-fours up on its end and Esther takes the other one, walking backward to unfurl the banner as Jesse turns her end around and around. When it's all the way open, Jesse leans around to look at it. In big red block letters on the gray background it says PEACE NOW.

A white Access-a-Ride van pulls up to the sidewalk, and the door puffs open. Esther props her end of the banner up on the folding chair and steps forward expectantly. The van beeps as the handicapped lift folds out from the open door like a giant diesel tongue. A tiny, white-haired lady in a velour tracksuit shuffles onto the lift, pushing a walker, and stands impassive while the lift grinds its way down and delivers her onto the sidewalk. Esther reaches out her arm and steadies Margaret as she inches forward off the platform.

"Good morning, good morning!" Margaret bellows in a throaty voice, thick with New York accent. She sounds like a cross between Fran Drescher on *The Nanny* and Jesse's grandpa, who spent his whole life in Brooklyn before retiring to Delray Beach, Florida, last year to live with his seventy-five-year-old girlfriend. "Good morning, gorgeous girls and boys!" Jesse isn't sure now what she was expecting Margaret to be like, but it wasn't this. She can't believe that huge voice could come out of such a miniature lady.

"Good morning, Margaret," Esther says, and hugs Margaret fervently, awkwardly, around her shoulders. Margaret reaches one gnarled hand up off the walker and pats Esther perfunctorily, then edges out of her embrace.

"Move aside, move aside, let the old man out." Margaret shuffles away from the van door and the lift repeats its performance, hoisting up and folding in, then lurching back down to the sidewalk, this time with a tall, stooped gentleman on it, hunched over his own walker. He's wearing a long, beige trench coat over sweatpants, and dress shoes with white socks, and when he reaches the sidewalk he calls back over his shoulder to the driver: "A thousand thanks, Bert!" The driver waves to Charlie, smiling wanly behind his mirrored sunglasses. "Poor Bert," Charlie comments to whoever might be listening. "That guy hates us. We torment that guy." Charlie's accent is more tart, more New England than Margaret's—he sounds a little like the old guy from the Pepperidge Farm ads.

"He doesn't hate *me*," Margaret objects. "Bert loves *me*. It's *you* he hates."

"He only hates me because he knows I'm right."

"He hates you because he has a route full of people to get to and you hold him hostage in our driveway for forty minutes at a time lecturing him about social security!"

Charlie leans in to Jesse. "He *pretends* to believe what they tell him on Fox News, but deep down inside he knows I'm right. That's why he hates me. Charlie Magnu-son." Charlie extends his hand to Jesse, and she takes it.

"Jesse Halberstam," Jesse says. Charlie's hand is big and dry and heavy, and it creaks a little in the wrist as she squeezes it.

"Of the Chicago Halberstams?" Charlie peers at Jesse as if trying to place her. His face is long and droopy, his wispy hair more sandy yellow than white. "Are you related by any chance to Morty Halberstam, attorney-at-law?"

Jesse shakes her head. "I don't think so."

"Find out," Charlie instructs her. "That guy is one in a million. Kept a good friend of mine out of prison."

"If he asks you a question, don't answer it," Margaret warns Jesse. "If you think of a question for him, don't ask it. Otherwise he'll start talking and never let you go." To Arlo, she says, "Hello, Arlo."

Arlo nods. "Margaret. Charlie."

"Chair, chair, chair," Margaret commands, and Esther helps her over to the nearer of the two folding chairs. Margaret lowers herself excruciatingly slowly toward the seat, then collapses the last few inches into a sitting position. "Not so long ago I could stand on my own two feet for an hour on a Sunday," she explains to Jesse. "But no longer. Now I sit down for peace. Ha! At least my ass is still on the line. Ha!" She laughs a big, loud laugh, and Charlie joins her. He's headed down to the chair at the far end of the banner. It takes him a minute, but he gets there, and once he's arranged himself in the chair he picks up his end of the banner and holds it upright. Esther hands Margaret the other end, and above them the big town clock begins to chime. *Gong, gong, gong, gong . . .*

"Forty-two years," Margaret says proudly. "Haven't missed a noontime yet."

Esther and Arlo and Jesse all choose signs from the grass behind the banner (Jesse picks NO TO WAR, which seems basic, and a true enough statement about how she feels) and hold them up. Margaret and Charlie each hold an end of the banner. And then they all stand there.

Cars pass. Across the street, a woman walks out of Jansen's with two small blond children, holding each by one hand, and goes into Beverly Coffee next door without even glancing across the street. More cars pass. Nobody says anything. The five of them just stand there and do nothing.

After a minute or so, Jesse starts to feel jumpy. She squeezes her toes and bounces a little inside her boots.

"Shouldn't we, like, chant or sing or something?" she asks Esther quietly.

"It's not a demonstration, gorgeous," Margaret explains loudly, as if Jesse had posed the question to her directly. "It's a vigil. You ever been to a vigil before?"

Jesse shakes her head.

"At a vigil, the point is not to make a bunch of noise and ruckus, the point is to stand up for what you believe in. Or in my case, sit down for what you believe in. Ha!"

"But um, what if no one pays attention to us?" Jesse asks. She hopes it's not a rude question. Across the street, shoppers are coming and going, and no one has stopped to acknowledge—even to look at—the little group with their placards only fifty feet away.

"They see us," Charlie says.

"They see us," Esther agrees vehemently.

"And even if they don't," Margaret continues, "the point is just to be here. To stand up and be counted for what's right."

As if on cue, a passing Ford Taurus honks its horn, and the driver waves out the window at them. Margaret, Charlie, and Esther wave back enthusiastically.

"Hey." Arlo has sidled over so he's right next to Jesse, on the far side from Esther, and he pokes her in the sleeve to get her attention.

"Hey." Jesse edges a fraction of an inch away from him.

"I get you," Arlo says in a low voice. "Believe me. I get your problem."

"My problem?"

"I hear what you're trying to say. It feels purely symbolic, right? Like we're not really *doing* anything? I hear you."

"I don't know if I—"

"Look, the first time someone dragged me here, I was like, this is the most pathetic thing I have ever seen. These people have been standing here on this corner for *forty years* begging, what, the air? and the sky? for peace? And *is* there peace? Did they make peace happen? The world's in worse shape than ever, man! If they want peace so bad, why don't they go chain themselves to a nuclear silo in Colorado or picket the White House or blow up the head-quarters of Halliburton—like you could even *find* the real headquarters of Halliburton, right?" Arlo chuckles con-spiratorially, and Jesse nods because she's not sure what else to do.

"'By any means necessary,' right? That's more your style?"

"I guess?"

"Yeah, that was me, too. I get you. I was all about di-rect action. And I wasn't afraid of violence. I was at the Battle in Seattle in '99, see?" Arlo drops his sign to the ground and tugs up the sleeve of his army jacket, revealing a crisscrossed network of pale, wormy scars running up and down his bony forearm. "Friendly fire," he says with unconcealed pride. "Bottle rocket, premature detonation. I was supposed to throw it at the limo carrying the head of the World Trade Organization, but I didn't time the fuse right. Went off in my hand, man."

Jesse looks down at the arm Arlo is thrusting into her face and nods politely. "Nice."

"Nice?" Arlo echoes, clearly offended. *"Nice?"*

"I just meant—"

"Is he showing you his scars?" Esther interrupts, leaning over Jesse now to peer at Arlo. "Arlo, are you forcing Jesse to look at your mangled arm? Put that away, nobody wants to see that."

"I'm not forcing anyone to do anything, I'm talking to the new girl about direct political action!"

"Stop trying to prove how tough you are and leave Jesse alone."

"It's okay, really. . . ." Sandwiched in between the hot intensity of Arlo and the cool intensity of Esther, Jesse starts to feel slightly claustrophobic.

"For your information, Esther, I was about to tell her that I put all that in the past, thanks to Margaret and Charlie and this group. I was about to tell her that I'm all about pure presence now and just being here in a peaceful way to bring about the new world order."

"All right, so now you've told her. Put your arm back in your jacket."

"You guys, it's cool, it's cool." Jesse just wants them to stop bickering. What is it with people getting into conflicts at peace rallies?

In a huff, Arlo shrugs his sleeve back down over his arm, then turns away to check his BlackBerry with his back to the group.

"He's right, though," Esther says to Jesse. "The point is just to be. You don't have to do anything besides be right here."

* * *

By 12:55, Jesse has counted about twenty-five people who have honked or waved in support of peace. First Jesse's right hand, then her left cramped up stiffly around the ruler handle taped to her NO TO WAR sign. Her feet have grown tingly from standing still so long. But she feels a kind of contented calm that she almost never feels. She can't remember the last time she just stood in one place and watched the world go by. It's surprising how few people she's seen that she knows, even in this town that always feels so small to her. A whole hour of standing in front of the Town Hall and she's recognized only a few people: Ms. Arocho from the library; Dr. Paul Klang, her dentist; Brianna from her dad's office. Other than that, it's all been brief flashes of people she doesn't know. Kids, babies, teenagers, parents. Couples, old ladies, college guys. People walking with shopping bags, people running in short-shorts and earphones, people feeding meters, people holding hands. Dogs, dogs, dogs. The sun is warm on Jesse's skin; the clouds skid smoothly across the blue overhead.

A low green hatchback covered in bumper stickers approaches and honks an enthusiastic rat-a-tattoo as it passes. Esther calls out, "Hi, Huckle!" and Huckle waves from the driver's seat. Margaret and Charlie and Esther wave. Jesse waves. Twenty-six people.

"Hard to believe this is all headed for the crapper, this beautiful little town," Arlo says darkly.

"That's right," Charlie grouses from the other end of the banner. He mutters: "Sonsofbitches."

"Why is it headed for the crapper?" Jesse asks. "Who are sons of bitches?"

"Don't ask him—" Margaret warns, but Charlie practically shouts over her, "Crooked town meeting members in the pocket of the big-box stores!"

"Don't start!" Margaret bosses him, then turns back to Jesse. "You can't mention StarMart within earshot of that man or he loses his mind. It makes him crazy how they're sleazeballing their way in."

"StarMart?" Jesse says. "But I thought they lost. I thought the Snope Christmas Tree Farm people said no."

StarMart, the mega-retailer, had recently attempted to buy up farmland out on Route 10 to convert into a giant one-stop discount store, a hot topic of conversation for months in the Halberstam house. Even though Fran and Arthur were in complete agreement about how terrible it would be for the town if a big-box store moved in, they managed to argue about who was more right about how awful the fallout would be, and who had the better points about the damage StarMart would do. It ended when the Snope family made the front page of the local paper by refusing to sell StarMart their land.

"You haven't heard?" Arlo says. "StarMart's new plan is to try to force the Snopes into selling by putting pressure on every part of the town. Town meeting. The schools. I heard a couple of selectboard members have been offered bribes. Even the Francis Animal Shelter got a call from somebody over at NorthStar, promising a lifetime's supply of Milk-Bones if NorthStar gets permission to build inside the town line. It's a PR onslaught."

"It's true," Esther agrees. "Ms. Filarski told me they're sponsoring a bunch of athletic teams at Vander and giving money to fund the dance that's coming up at school."

"They figure if they make the deal irresistible enough to the town, people will put the screws to Frank and Jane Snope until they give in." Charlie shakes his head in disgust.

"That's why Charlie and I are starting a grassroots anti-StarMart organization," Arlo says. "Right, Charlie? What are we calling it again?"

"People for the Preservation of Safe Small Towns. PPSST."

"Wait, no, I thought it was FASST: Fighting Against Sprawl in Small Towns."

"No, it was PPSST."

"I think it was definitely FASST, or possibly Americans Against Unrestrained Retailer Growth? AAURG?"

"We haven't come to consensus yet about a name, but we're going to put the hurt to those sonsofbitches as soon as we decide on a name, you mark my words! If that store gets built it'll be like all the other towns in America whose lifeblood has been drained out of them by bloodsucking multinational corporations!"

"All right, all right," Margaret shouts him down. "Pipe down, darling!" To Jesse, she remarks, "I told you, he can't stay calm when he talks about it. His doctor says it's a stroke risk, and he's not supposed to discuss it."

"You like Main Street?" Charlie shouts, undeterred. "You like free trade and little stores and local business? Well, kiss it good-bye! Kiss it *all* good-bye if StarMart sinks their hooks into this town!"

Charlie waves his hand dramatically over the street in front of him, gesturing to all that will be lost.

Jesse turns to look at the doomed downtown, and just at that moment he rounds the corner and heads up the block: Mike McDade, ambling easy through the afternoon in his khakis, button-down shirt, and baseball cap. Mike McDade, the square-jawed. Mike McDade, the broad-shouldered. Mike McDade, the six-foot-one, all-American shortstop. Mike McDade, the love of Jesse's love's life.

Jesse watches him, transfixed.

The guy walks like nothing has ever stood in his way or fallen in his path, like his body has never encountered the slightest resistance in the world. He moves like some-one who has never been anything but welcomed wher-ever he's gone. His stride is long, his hands are loose and comfortable in his pockets, his chin is up, he seems to be . . . whistling? Mike McDade is freaking whistling. Because that's just how zip-a-dee-doo-dah he feels.

This is how he always looks. It's how he looks when he's walking Emily down the senior hall, his big, broad hand floating lightly over the small of her back. It's how he looks when he's leaning beside her locker looking down at her, or slinging his long arm over her shoulders, or fake-punching her affectionately on the shoulder, or bending down to kiss her in the door to her math class. He looks easy. Relaxed. *Satisfied.* Mike McDade is living his perfect life.

Without noticing the posse of peaceniks across the street, Mike tugs open the door to Murray and Sons Hardware and disappears inside. Jesse hears the faint, distant tinkle of the bell as the door falls shut.

"I mean, right? Hey, new girl, right?" Suddenly, Jesse is aware that Arlo is speaking to her, has been speaking to her for some time now.

"I'm sorry," she says. "I spaced for a second. What were you saying?"

"Who were you watching over there?" Arlo asks, his voice low and confidential.

"Nobody, I was just . . . zoning."

"Come on, you were watching someone. Who? You can tell me."

Jesse sighs. "My nemesis," she admits.

"You have a nemesis?" Arlo says. *"Excellent."*

* * *

Twenty minutes later, Jesse is sitting wedged into the backseat of her mother's Camry with an uncomfortable heap of peace signs in her lap, and her cheek pressed against the gritty two-by-four of the *Peace Now* banner. The only way it would fit into the compact car was diagonally inside, so that Jesse is stuffed in on one side of it in the backseat, and Esther has the other end resting heavily on her shoulder in the front seat.

Her mom had been pulling out of the parking lot with Jesse in the passenger seat beside her when they both simultaneously spotted Esther, trying to manage the heavy banner under one arm and keep ahold of the whole mess of signs under the other. When she told them she was heading for the bus stop to ride home, Fran told Jesse to get out of the car and help Esther in.

"So how was it, you guys?" Jesse's mom asks now, over-eager. "You get a lot of important things accomplished?"

"The point of a peace vigil isn't to get things accomplished, it's just to *be* there," Jesse snaps. Even she's aware of how obnoxious she sounds.

"Pardonnez-moi," Fran says mock-delicately. "Did you do a lot of good 'being there' then?"

"Oh yes," Esther says sincerely. "It was excellent. It's excellent every week."

"You go to the vigil every week?" Fran inquires. Jesse can see her surveying Esther curiously out of the corner of her eye.

"Yeah, for the past two years I've been going pretty much every week. I really like the people. Some of them I know from other places, like I work with Phyllis at the soup kitchen, and Louis runs the after-school program for kids where I volunteer tutor. Arlo keeps trying to get me to help out with his anarchist freegan cooperative over in Cold River, but I'm not so interested in what they do. He's really nice, though, usually." Esther cranes her neck around to address Jesse in the backseat. "He was just trying to show off for you by being tough because you were new."

"I didn't mind him," Jesse says truthfully.

"And is it still basically Margaret and Charlie's show over there?" Fran asks.

Esther whips around to face Fran—as far around as she can turn beneath the two-by-fours—her face alive with anticipation and joy. "You know Margaret and Charlie?" Jesse has never seen Esther so openly filled with emotion.

Jesse thinks, *Mom, you knew about the vigil?*

"Sure, from the old days. I must have been on a hundred marches with those two. What are they, pushing eighty by now? They're indefatigable. Fatiguing to others, perhaps, but indefatigable themselves."

"I know, aren't they *incredible*?" Esther gushes. "I consider them my honorary grandparents. I wish I could move in with them."

"Wow." Fran nods.

"I've never met *anyone* more committed to social justice than Margaret and Charlie, have you?" Esther speaks fiercely.

Fran raises her eyebrows. "I . . ."

"I want to be just like them when I grow up. They never stop learning new things, they're always figuring out what the next problem is they need to tackle. Like just today they were talking about trying to stop StarMart from moving into town. Do you know about that?"

"Absolutely," Fran says. "I was just reading in the paper that they haven't gone away since Frank and Jane refused to sell, they've just adjusted their strategy. They're bad bad bad, those guys. Major-league baddies. They ruin local economies and abuse their workers. And Jess, they give money to antigay political candidates; you of all people should hit the barricades for this one."

"We need to work on this," Esther asserts, fully energized now. "Jesse and I are starting our own peace and social justice organization and we were looking for a project to collaborate on. This is perfect!"

"You two have formed an organization?"

"Not officially," Jesse says hastily. "Informally."

"Jesse has agreed to lend the marketing skills she's developed as part of NOLAW to help my new organization, SPAN, improve its outreach to the student body."

Fran smiles. "I feel a little like I'm at a UN subcommittee meeting and I don't have my translator headphones on," she says. "SPAN? NOLAW? Fill me in here, please."

"Well, you know NOLAW," Esther says brightly, "Jesse's organization that produces the funny manifestos?"

"I'm afraid I don't. Tell me more."

Jesse leans her head back and closes her eyes.

"You don't know about Jesse's hilarious manifestos that she puts up copies of all over school every few weeks?"

"I do not. But I'm starting to get a sense of why my toner bill has been so astronomical lately."

"Jesse, I can't believe you haven't shown your mom your manifestos. They're so wonderful. I'm sure she'd love them."

"I'm sure I would."

"And SPAN is my organization, Student Peace Action Network, and now Jesse and I are joining forces, and this is just perfect for us. Hey, Jesse, if they're sponsoring the dance that's coming up, why don't we do some kind of action to disrupt that?"

"I don't know if a Vander dance is the greatest place for an action," Jesse says. "I've been to one. It was incredibly stupid."

Fran raises her eyebrows in surprise. "When did you go to a school dance?"

"Last year, I went to one for like five minutes, I told you about it."

"You never told me that."

"I'm sure I told you. Maybe I forgot. Whatever. Dances are totally gender-oppressive and awful."

"Well, maybe we don't have to actually go to the dance to disrupt it, maybe we can just try to prevent StarMart from sponsoring it or something. Why don't you come over to my house and we can do some research and plan out our strategy?"

"Great idea!" says Fran overheartily. Jesse gives the back of her head a quizzical look.

"Sure," Jesse says.

"Like, Tuesday? After school?"

"I can't Tuesday. What about Saturday?"

"Yeah, if I don't have ASP. I probably won't; I'm not planning any in-school actions this week."

"I'll drive you," Fran interjects.

"That's cool, Mom. I can take the bus or whatever."

"Well, I'll pick you up when you're done, then."

"Thanks, Mom. But chill."

When Esther goes to get out of the car, Fran leans over and shakes her hand.

"I have to say, Esther, it's been very educational meeting you. I've learned so many new things about my daughter in such a short time. Apparently, she goes to dances, runs political organizations—"

"Yeah, thanks for the vigil," Jesse says, cutting her mother off. "I'll see you next Saturday, Esther. Or before that, in school."

After Esther has extracted herself and her equipment from the car, made it up the long, narrow concrete steps to her house, and disappeared through her front door, Jesse climbs into the front seat next to her mother. Fran sits there for a moment with the key in the ignition but the Camry turned off.

"You're quite the sly one," she says to Jesse, smirking.

"Yeah, I'm sorry about the toner, I just—"

"I'm talking about your clever move: 'Oh I have to go to the peace vigil, I want to become more politically active.' You like that girl, don't you!" Fran grins. "You came to the vigil to get closer to her!"

"Oh my God, no I didn't!" Jesse howls.

"I love it! It's the oldest trick in the book! You're a chip off the old block, if I may say."

"You've got it all wrong, Mother."

"Or do I have it all *right*?" Jesse's mother looks immensely pleased with herself. "Listen, I'm just delighted that, first of all, I figured this out by myself, and second of all, you picked such a fantastic girl to have a crush on. That Esther is enthusiastic, smart, up on current events— she's a keeper, I can tell."

"Mom—"

"And you guys obviously make a great team."

"Mom, start the car."

Fran turns the engine on but keeps the Camry in park.

"I just want to say for the record," she says seriously, "that the only thing I want is for you to be happy."

"I *know*—"

"No, listen, will you listen to me for once in your life? I know you make jokes about me and Daddy being the oppressor, but you do know that we love and accept you exactly the way you are, don't you?"

"Yes." Jesse sighs impatiently.

"We never want you to have to hide anything from us or be secretive about any part of your life. That's not what we want for you, all right?"

A slow misery works its way through Jesse's bloodstream. She nods, and looks out the window at Esther's small blue house, at its darkened windows. It looks like no one is home. She can't turn back to look at her mother, or she's afraid she'll start to cry.

"Anytime you want to bring the girl you like home to meet us, we would absolutely love to have her."

If I brought home the girl I actually like, Jesse thinks, her heart shrinking at the center of her body, *you would be so, so disappointed in me.*

"Thanks, Mom," Jesse says. "I know."

10

Emily

It was no picnic figuring out how to fit the NorthStar internship into my schedule this late in the semester. I have work at the library on Tuesdays and student council on Wednesdays, and having me home to help prepare family dinner is really important to my mom on Fridays, so those are all non-negotiables, and Mr. Willette wanted me at least two afternoons a week, so I had no choice but to move my Monday Mandarin lessons (thank God Li Feng was flexible) and regretfully resign from Stonington General Hospital's prestigious and hard-to-get-into Apprentice Nursing Assistant program, which includes a non-negotiable commitment every Thursday.

I *so* dreaded calling Ms. Cheesewright, who runs the program. I was putting it off and putting it off all weekend, but finally my mom was like, "The longer you wait, the worse it'll be," and I was like, You're so right, and then she was like, "Like pulling off a Band-Aid: quick and firm." So I gathered all my courage and called Ms. Cheesewright and told her quickly and firmly that very unfortunately something non-negotiable had come up and I had to drop out of Apprentice Nursing Assistants. She was not thrilled to hear it. First she was like, "Emily, are you aware of how positively this program is looked upon by college admissions offices? You'll be doing yourself a tremendous disservice by not participating," and I was like, I know but I'm sorry, I very unfortunately have to resign, and then she was like, "Emily, are you aware of how many highly qualified young people applied to this program and were turned down? People who would never dream of giving up a spot midway through the semester?" and I was like, Yes I know and I'm really, really sorry but something non-negotiable has come up and I very unfortunately have to seriously resign.

Afterward I was, like, shaking. For a second, right after I put the phone down, I thought I might throw up. I *hate* letting people down. It's my least favorite thing in the *world*. My mom was so sweet to me about it, though—she made me tea and sat with me on the couch and reminded me that this experience was actually really good practice for me. She said it's a really important life skill to be able to gracefully tell someone that you can't do something for them. If you don't learn how to do it early on, you can get bogged down your whole life doing things for other people that don't benefit you, just because you feel bad telling them no. She said it's a thing that women in particular have to struggle with. Later on that night, I found an article on my pillow that she had torn out of *O,* Oprah's magazine, that's all about this problem, how women get trapped in what the article calls "Prisons of Good Intentions" and just endlessly do things for other people instead of doing what's best for them, and how it ruins their lives and makes them angry, resentful people. That's certainly not the kind of person I want to be.

And as awful as that phone call and that whole weekend was, after my first day at NorthStar, I can confidently say that it was totally, completely worth it.

I had an incredible afternoon. First of all, right when I got there, Mr. Willette showed me the desk where I'll be working, which is in a corner of the reception area outside his and Ms. Rinaldi's offices, and which is dark mahogany wood grain with a padded, light blue office chair, a desktop computer, and a combination scanner/printer/fax machine I'll use to assist with NorthStar Enterprises' corporate communications. There's a locked drawer in the desk for me to keep my personal belongings in when I'm not in the office, and Mr. Willette gave me the tiny key to it to take with me on my key ring.

Then he took me on a tour of the entire space. It's a pretty quiet, serious workplace, not loud and friendly like my dad's office at Independent Fiduciary Research and Management, where all of the offices are arranged around one big open area, and some of the investment managers have TVs on in their offices to keep track of the markets, and the secretaries all listen to different light FM stations on radios under their desks and yell to each other across the room whenever they see something funny on the Internet.

The NorthStar office is way smaller, first of all—only about twenty-five people work there total—and it feels more like an underground den, with long, dim, carpeted corridors leading to more long, dim, carpeted corridors and offices and restrooms and supply closets coming off them, and a break room and a conference room with frosted-glass walls. I didn't get to see inside the conference room because they were having a meeting when we passed it, but Mr. Willette showed me all around the break room. I can put any personal perishables I bring with me in a designated area of the fridge, and they have unlimited coffee, tea, and snacks for the employees, which I'm more than welcome to help myself to anytime I'd like. I didn't really get time to see what kinds of snacks there were in the little basket on the counter, but I'll go back on Thursday and check it out—*if* I can find my way back there! All the corridors at NorthStar look almost exactly the same, and I would have been so lost getting back to my desk from the break room if Mr. Willette hadn't personally led me there himself.

The whole office is decorated with this series of beautiful framed posters with photographs of tranquil nature scenes above poetic messages about doing your best work and making the most of your opportunities. The one right above my desk has a picture of three flying geese silhouetted against this huge, violet-colored moon rising over a lake, and underneath the picture it says YOU CAN SOAR ONLY AS HIGH AS YOU BELIEVE THE SKY TO BE. I wrote this down on a Post-it note and stuck it on the inside cover of my homework journal for inspiration.

It was really just an introductory day for me to get to get my feet wet and start meeting people, Mr. Willette said. Ms. Rinaldi did train me on the large-scale photocopier—which is huger and more complicated than any copier I've ever seen, it's like a tank or a robot hippopotamus or something—and she left me in charge of running off a series of reports in time for a late afternoon meeting, which stressed me out for a second, but which I managed to accomplish just fine. But other than that I didn't do any real work.

Still. Even though I wasn't completing any specific tasks, just *being* there I felt like I was doing something real. I don't even know how to explain it, but everywhere you go in that office, even when you can't see anyone working, you can *feel* that people are getting things done. People are making decisions. They're making things happen. Mr. Willette reminded me today that it may look like a small operation over there, but I am now working at the regional corporate headquarters of the third-largest retail company in the *world*. The mission of the company is to bring affordable, high-quality products to people who might not otherwise be able to get them, all over the planet. Every day, 163 million people from all different faiths, nationalities, creeds, and colors walk through the doors of a NorthStar Enterprises store. The decisions people make in this one office, in this one town, in this one state, could go on to affect 163 million people. It's so overwhelming, I can barely get my mind around it. It fills me with a crazy kind of pride.

Not that it's the same, but it reminds me a little bit of the time when I proposed the format change at the student council meetings. Before the change, there wasn't any kind of order for how the meetings ran, people just raised their hands and brought up whatever topics occurred to them—complaints or proposals or comments or whatever. It was fine, but it felt like we could never tackle anything big, because as soon as we'd start to really dig into a problem, someone would raise their hand and take us off on some random tangent and we'd never get back to the issue we started with. I proposed a new system where we began every meeting with a typed-up agenda of action items, so that we could go down the list in order and really make sure every item got addressed before we moved on to the next one. It seems like such a simple thing, but that small change made such a huge difference in the way student council meetings ran. The energy got totally efficient, and even though we were getting way more things done, our meetings actually went down from two hours to an hour and a half, on average. And every minute we were in that room together, it felt like something was actually happening. It feels like that in the NorthStar offices, but, like, 163 million times more.

I called Michael after I got home, and he picked me up to go celebrate my first day with ice cream at Twin Teddies Drive-In. Michael's favorite thing in the world is soft-serve and it's almost the end of the season and he won't be able to get it anymore for six months, so that's why I suggested Twin Teddies for our celebration. Personally, I'd always prefer Beverly Coffee or Panera at the mall, but I wanted to make Michael happy—he's done so much to make me happy. And he *was* totally happy. He got an extra-large twist cone with rainbow sprinkles, as tall and big around as a thermos, and ate the whole thing in, like, four monster bites. While he was eating, I told him everything about the afternoon at NorthStar, and the thing about the 163 million people across the globe. I told him that pretty soon I could be helping with decisions that will make it possible for people in, like, Bangladesh or Honduras to buy products that will improve their quality of life in ways they never imagined. And he gave me the sweetest look, not like his usual sweet look but a new, more bashful look, like he was just meeting me for the first time and was too nervous even to look me in the eye. He told me super-seriously that I am an inspiration to him. He said he's never known anyone else who cared as much as I do about making a difference. He said he felt lucky to be the one who loves me.

Sometimes that boy is so sweet, I swear, it makes my heart ache. It makes my stomach feel queasy. It makes me feel a little like I'm coming down with something.

That night I had the most vivid dream, the kind that leaves you surrounded by a fog of feeling for hours after you wake up out of it. I dreamt that it was the end of the day and I was leaving my job at NorthStar, which I had had for a long time in the dream, and I was incredibly psyched because I had made some really important decision about the company that day and everybody was really excited about it. And I drove home to my house (which turned out to be a sort of giant pumpkin with windows on stilts, but whatever), and as I was driving I thought, *I can't wait to tell Michael about the important decision!* But when I pulled into the driveway, it was Jesse waiting for me there on the porch, wearing only Michael's green-plaid bathrobe that his brother brought him home from UPenn and these fuzzy pink socks. In the dream, I realized that we lived there together, in the pumpkin house. I was so excited to see her that I jumped out of the car and ran toward her, leaving the car door open behind me. I couldn't wait to have my arms around her. As I was running I called out to her, like, almost crying with happiness, "I'm so glad you got rid of those *boots*!" And she laughed out loud, which she almost never does in real life, and said, "I did it because I love you."

And then I woke up. It was only 5:10 a.m., but I couldn't get back to sleep. My heart was racing. I just lay there wide awake for forty-five minutes feeling the thrill of running toward her move through me. I lay there listening to her voice in my mind, saying over and over again: *I love you. I love you.*

When I saw her in the hallway between third and fourth periods—we sometimes pass each other when she's coming from Spanish at one end of the junior hall and I'm coming from chem at the other end—I felt the dream flood through me again, and without even thinking about it, totally unconsciously, I called out, "Jesse!" But she rushed right past me. She didn't even look my way.

To be fair, we don't usually make eye contact at school. I guess she wasn't used to hearing me use her name.

It was just as well she didn't stop, because I was walking with Grace Gerena and Kimmie Hersh and I only got away with it because they were busy comparing their chem quizzes right then. If they hadn't been distracted, what would I have done? What would I have done if Jesse had stopped? What did I think I was going to do, right there in the middle of passing period, right there in front of everybody? Tell her that I loved her, too?

11

Jesse

When Esther opens her front door on Saturday morning, the first thing that hits Jesse is the smell. It smells like a pet store or a zoo: the yeasty, sawdusty odor of a caged animal and the nest it lives in. Involuntarily, Jesse backs up a step on the narrow porch to escape it, but Esther smiles her wide smile and says, "Hey, come in."

"Thanks," says Jesse, and steps inside.

It's so dark inside Esther's low-ceilinged house that it takes Jesse's eyes a second to adapt. After a moment, she makes out, through an arched doorway to her left, a living room drenched in murk, thick brown shades pulled down over the windows, one small lamp casting a pool of stained yellow light in the far corner. The room is heaped—*heaped*—all over with piles and piles and piles of stuff, some of it reaching almost all the way to the ceiling. There are cascading stacks of newspapers, wads of fabric (clothes? sheets? tablecloths? towels?), windup toys, coffee mugs, leaning towers of paperback books, abandoned dishes, a stepladder, shoe boxes full of lightbulbs and extension cords, a porcelain figurine of two swans kissing, a toaster on top of a turned-off TV. In the corner is an old-fashioned bonnet hair dryer that looks like a combination chaise longue and electric chair—a cracked vinyl seat with a silver helmet attached to an extension arm above it. Somewhere under the mountains of stuff, there seem to be a sofa and a couple of armchairs, but the furniture is just a suggestion under the drifts of objects—the hint of land under a heavy snow.

"The kitchen's this way," Esther says mildly, as if she hadn't just ushered Jesse into one of the most astonishing houses she's ever seen in her life. "I thought we could get a snack and then go up to my room to work."

"Yeah, sure."

"We can go up the back stairs from the kitchen." Esther leads Jesse along the narrow path that snakes through the overstuffed living room. "And don't worry about my dad, he's fine."

Only then does Jesse notice that there's a man on the couch, inches away from where she's standing. He's curled up on his side with his back facing the room, wedged into the crush of afghans, pillows, and magazines that cram the sofa: a sleeping giant in a nest of stuff. In a startled moment, Jesse takes in the curved, sharp knobs of his spine through his T-shirt, the droopy behind of his boxer shorts, the dirty soles of his long, white sweatsocks. He shifts a little as they pass and lets out a rumbling sleep-sigh. Jesse hurries after Esther, away from his too-live, shuddering body.

"He's just napping," Esther says, her voice light but a little strained.

"Oh yeah," says Jesse. "Yeah."

"I know it's kind of a mess, sorry," Esther continues. "I didn't really get a chance to clean up before you came."

"Kind of a mess?" Jesse thinks. *It would take a week of solid work to clean this place up.* But she says only, "No, it's fine."

They pass through a dining room as cavelike as the living room—it seems that there must be a table and chairs in there, but it's hard for Jesse to tell because of the mixed-up mass of board games, bottles, books, and table lamps that's piled on top of them—and into the kitchen, which is brighter, more open. The kitchen walls are yellow, the windows are dressed with little white café curtains, and although every surface is covered with crumbs and smears and sticky rings, and the sink is piled high with dirty dishes, at least there's one little breakfast table that's clear, not smothered in newspapers and junk. Jesse realizes that she's been sort of holding her breath since the moment she walked into Esther's house. She inhales now, and the faint perfume of sour milk fills her nose.

"Peanut butter and jelly okay?" Esther asks. Peanut

butter and jelly—particularly peanut butter and jelly made by someone else in a strange, messy kitchen—is one of the grossest snacks Jesse can imagine. But she says vaguely, "Yeah, sure, great."

Esther moves around the kitchen briskly, unself-consciously. She swipes up a filmy juice glass and a cereal bowl with a leftover pool of milk and floating Cheerios in it off the countertop and fits them in, Jenga-style, to the tower of dishes in the sink. Then she gets to work pulling plates, knives, and sandwich ingredients out of the cabinets and fridge.

"I'm glad you came over," Esther mentions to the countertop, not looking at Jesse.

Jesse waits for Esther to explain why it's helpful or practical or useful to have Jesse there. When she doesn't add anything after a moment, Jesse answers, "Yeah, me too."

In her pocket, Jesse feels her phone buzz. She checks it quickly: Wyatt. *Not now,* she thinks, and dismisses the call.

Unsure of what to do with herself, Jesse stands in front of the big mustard-yellow fridge and peruses its surface. The fridge door is a cheery collage of photos, receipts, menus from local restaurants, and happy magnets (an apple with a grinning, googly-eyed worm coming out of it, a blue plastic thermometer in the shape of the state of Michigan, a pig with a bandanna on its head and the words GO

HOG WILD! painted on its pink side), but as she peers at it longer, Jesse gets the funny sense that this fridge is a kind of museum exhibit—no one has stuck anything new up here for a long, long time. One of the menus tacked under the map of Michigan is for Martinelli's Pizza, which closed at least two years ago; Bedazzlers Nail Salon is there now, where Jesse's mom gets her only-in-the-summertime pedicures. All of the photographs on the fridge are of Esther, but she's no more than ten or eleven years old in any of them. There's five-year-old Esther in a little green two-piece bathing suit at the beach, squinting seriously and holding up a pink plastic shovel. There's eight-year-old Esther in a snowsuit and mittens, grinning and shaking the stick-hand of a tipsy-looking, half-melted snowman. There's a school picture of Esther from maybe sixth grade, her braids in exactly the same disarray as they are now, her eyes wide—almost startled—above her broad, tiny-toothed smile.

"You're so cute in these pictures," Jesse offers, but Esther doesn't respond. She's working on the sandwiches with what Jesse now recognizes is her customary intensity, digging into the peanut butter jar as if she's stabbing a wild animal, then spreading the peanut butter so fiercely that the bread tears a little under the attack of her knife. Her lips move as she reaches for the jelly, around silent words that Jesse can't make out.

Jesse's phone buzzes again against her thigh, and she

reaches in to get rid of the call without even taking it out of her pocket.

When the two tattered sandwiches are ready, Esther leads Jesse up the back stairs to her room. Jesse's bracing for it to be a dark, claustrophobic den like the downstairs, but it turns out to be tidy and light, with slanted ceilings, dormer windows, packed-tight bookshelves against almost every wall, and a big area over her desk that's wallpapered with overlapping images, all of them old-fashioned paintings of girls on horseback, girls pointing into the future, girls holding swords, girls sobbing, girls praying, girls with halos, girls lashed with rope to wooden stakes, girls surrounded by angels.

"Who are all those girls?" Jesse asks, drawn to the wall.

"That's all one girl." Esther looks at Jesse warily. "That's Joan of Arc."

"Oh."

"You know about Joan of Arc, right?" Esther sets the sandwiches down and turns on her clunky old desktop computer. It beeps twice, loud and angry, and whirrs to life, the screen blinking awake.

"Sort of." Jesse smiles apologetically.

"You don't know about Joan of Arc?"

Jesse shrugs. "I mean, basically."

"How can you not know about Joan of Arc?" Esther almost shouts, then sighs dramatically. "I guess I shouldn't be surprised, hardly anybody really knows about her. But you of all *people* should know about Joan!"

"Why me of all people?"

Esther sputters. "Uh, because she was a girl soldier who dressed like a boy and led an army of rebels into battle?"

"That sounds awesome."

"It was awesome! It's ridiculous that you don't know about her. I get so upset when people don't know her story." Shaking her head in exasperation, Esther crosses to the bookshelf by her bed and pulls out a long, slim hardback picture book. It's slightly warped and lightly browned at the edges. In 1920s-style Art Deco lettering, it says *Joan of Arc: The Story of a Saint* on the cover. "Take this home and read it," Esther commands, and Jesse accepts the book. "If she's not your new personal idol by the time you're done with this book, I'll . . ."

"What?" Jesse challenges her, smiling.

Esther doesn't smile. "I don't know, but it'll be a serious problem between us. And please be extremely careful with this book when you handle it. It's an antique."

"Oh. Okay." Tentatively, with as much care as she can muster, Jesse goes to open the book, but Esther reaches out and pinches it shut.

"Not now," she instructs. "We have research to do. Put it away in your bag."

Wordlessly, Jesse does as she's told. As she slips the

book into her backpack, Esther settles herself at the desk in front of her computer.

In her pocket, Jesse's phone buzzes a third time.

"Do you have to get that?" Esther asks a little impatiently. "Someone obviously really wants to talk to you."

Jesse opens her phone just long enough to see that it's Wyatt before she shuts it off.

"No," she says. "It's no one. I'm turning it off."

"All right." Esther clicks open her Internet browser and chuckles a little. "We're coming for you, StarMart," she says with unusual relish.

Jesse is delighted. "You sound like an evil villain."

"Oh no," corrects Esther, turning to Jesse with her dead serious look on again. "They're the villains. We're the heroes of this story."

✳ ✳ ✳

What the Internet will teach you about StarMart:

One: That the reason it can sell its products so cheaply (only three dollars for a shirt?!) is because it manufactures them in places in the world like Bangladesh or Honduras where the laws are so unfair to workers that you can get away with paying people only a few cents a day for ten hours of work in a hot, filthy factory.

Two: That even here in the US, StarMart pays its employees so poorly that more than half of them are on welfare or have to get food stamps or other government assistance. They can't afford to pay for basic food and medical care, even though they're working full-time for StarMart. And any time the workers in one StarMart store try to come together and form a union so they can bargain for better wages, the company threatens to close down the store, or just fires them all and replaces them with new underpaid workers.

Three: That NorthStar Enterprises—which is the big company that runs all of the StarMart and StarBasket Select and ShootingStar Bulk Shopping Club stores—gives tons of money to conservative politicians who make laws that benefit big businesses. Their biggest contribution every year in this area is to State Senator Candace Reese-Allen, who famously cast the deciding vote against legalizing gay marriage and who was quoted in the paper as saying that gay people are "biological errors" who are "dangerous to society" and "hateful to God."

Four: That when a StarMart moves to the outskirts of your town, it quickly drives all the small stores in the center of town out of business, because they can't afford to compete with StarMart's insanely low prices. A lot of times, after StarMart has moved in and killed all the family-owned businesses in one town, they'll close down that store and open a new one in the next town over, because the new town will offer them fresh bonuses and tax breaks to build a new store. And the first town is left with nothing: no small businesses, no StarMart. A ghost town where a thriving community used to be.

Five: That StarMart opens a new store somewhere in the world every two days.

Jesse and Esther sit, stunned, staring at the computer.

"They're like . . . the Death Star of stores," Jesse murmurs. "It's like they only exist to ruin people's towns and take their money. It's like they don't even care what they do to the world."

"Corporations don't have consciences," Esther explains. "They don't have souls. They don't care about things. They only exist for one purpose: to make money."

"Well, we can't let that money touch our school. I mean, clearly. We need a plan."

"Posters," Esther says.

"Posters," Jesse echoes. She opens her notebook to a blank page to start taking notes for ideas.

"We'll make them yellow, the StarMart color. And we need to go to the next student council meeting and make a presentation."

Jesse's stomach lurches.

"Student council? Do we have to?"

"Of course. They're the ones running the dance, aren't they? The 'Official StarMart Prom Night,' or whatever it's called now?"

"'Starry Starry Night,'" Jesse says dully, recalling the

flyers announcing the dance that went up around school at the end of the week.

Jesse looks down at the floor, picks listlessly at the braided rags in Esther's rug. She pictures herself standing in a room full of student council kids, all looking at her while she looks at Emily. She pictures Emily at the center of the room, giving Jesse her brightest blank smile, banging her gavel on the desk to make Jesse sit down and shut up.

"Right. So if it's their dance, we have to go talk to them about it," Esther says patiently. "Obviously."

"Can't we just go directly to the principal?"

"If we start by going to Mr. Greil's office alone, just the two of us, we won't have any power. We need to develop awareness and solidarity among the student body. We should really start a petition. Oh! We'll start a petition!" Esther bounces a little in her desk chair with excitement. "The student council meeting is the perfect place for us to start getting the word out about it."

"I just . . ." Jesse feels two tides moving through her simultaneously, a surge of wanting to tell someone about Emily—an urgent, almost physical wave of needing to confess—and a grinding-to-a-halt feeling in her throat, as if her words are drying up and evaporating before they can even reach her tongue. "I just . . . I just . . ." she struggles.

"Do you have some kind of allergy to the student council? Why don't you want to go to this meeting?" Esther looks at her with open curiosity.

"I just . . . hate public speaking," Jesse says finally, unconvincingly.

"Oh," Esther says. "Well, fine. I mean, Mother Teresa used to be afraid of public speaking and she got over it, but that's fine. I'll do all the talking. You can just stand there and hand out literature." It's a compromise; Jesse doesn't see how she can keep objecting once Esther offers this.

"Okay," she agrees.

"Okay. So first thing Monday morning we'll put up posters with, like, bullet points about StarMart and their relationship to Vander, saying that everybody who wants to learn more should come to this week's student council meeting. Then we'll write up an information sheet with all the facts on it that we can hand to people when they come to the meeting on Wednesday. Then we'll start a petition that we can bring to Mr. Greil."

"Cool." Jesse nods. "That's cool. It's a lot of work, though."

"Yes, I like to work," Esther says briskly. "I like to do anything that gets me out of the house."

WAKE UP, VANDER!
SERIOUSLY!

Say NO to StarMart in Our School!

DID YOU KNOW that StarMart
is trying to move into our town?

DID YOU KNOW that when StarMart moves into a
town, it makes local businesses close down, takes good
jobs away from people, and is bad for the environment?

DID YOU KNOW that StarMart uses unfair sweatshop
labor in poor countries to make its cheap products?

DID YOU KNOW THAT STARMART HAS STRUCK
A DEAL TO PAY FOR SOME OF VANDER'S ATHLETIC
EXPENSES AND ALSO THIS YEAR'S FALL FORMAL?

**DANCING AT THE STARMART FALL FORMAL IS LIKE
DANCING ON THE BACKS OF SWEATSHOP WORKERS!**

**DANCING AT THE STARMART FALL FORMAL IS LIKE
DANCING ON THE GRAVES OF LOCAL BUSINESSES!**

IS THAT THE KIND OF DANCING

YOU
WANT TO DO???

LET STUDENT COUNCIL KNOW HOW YOU FEEL!

COME TO THE MEETING ON WEDNESDAY!

OR GO TO WWW.SPRAWLWATCH.NET!

STARMART OUT OF VANDER NOW!

12

Jesse

Jesse hovers a little ways down the hall from the door to Room A23 at 2:42 p.m. on Wednesday, half waiting impatiently for Esther to show up, and half trying to pretend that what's about to happen isn't actually about to happen. Her whole body is buzzing with a fizzy mix of terror and eagerness; she bounces up and down and flexes her toes inside her boots, using every spare centimeter of wiggle room they allow. The student council meeting is supposed to start at 2:45. T minus three minutes to Emily vs. Esther.

It's all gone according to plan so far. The posters went up super early on Monday morning—Jesse and Esther managed to slip into school at the crack of dawn with the custodians, so they were able to sweep through the building unhindered by Snediker, blitzing posters onto every wall with rapid, preplanned precision. (No precious seconds were lost fumbling for tape this time—Jesse came prepared with two rolls of it clipped to her belt loop on a carabiner, like a Boy Scout going for his Office Supplies badge.) By the time first period was over on Monday, the whole school was humming lightly with talk about StarMart, kids questioning each other in the halls about the dance, Mr. Kennerley bringing it up as a case study in Jesse's social studies class. Between sixth and seventh periods, Esther caught Jesse's eye in the hall and flashed her a thrilling, significant smile—*StarMart out of Vander NOW!* had already become a couple kids' status updates, and Jesse could feel the whole thing simmering, gathering steam, about to take off.

But on Monday night, Jesse lay in bed wide awake for hours, her eyes glazed open, her mind racing with thoughts about Emily. Around and around she went. First she thought, *I have to warn her. I have to tell her that I'm about to come in and bomb her next student council meeting.* Then she thought, *No, she's not going to love that I'm doing this.* Then: *Maybe Esther's right—maybe Emily will totally be on our side once she finds out the truth about StarMart. Maybe she's already decided to cut StarMart out of the dance now that she's seen the posters!* And then: *What am I thinking, remember the Handi Snak incident? There's no way Emily's going to let StarMart go so easily.* And then finally: *Anyway, what if I tell her what we're doing and she refuses to kiss me? What if she refuses to ever kiss me again? I can't tell her. I have to tell her. I can't tell her.*

By Tuesday afternoon, when Jesse arrived at the hand-icapped bathroom on the second floor of the Minot Library, she was practically wall-eyed with sleep deprivation and panic. But in the end, the decision was made for her. The moment she saw Emily, the moment Emily reached for her hand, the words *I have to tell you something* vaporized from Jesse's tongue. The only thing to do, it seemed to Jesse then, was to slip into Emily's arms, pull out Emily's ponytail, kiss down Emily's open throat, and stay quiet.

Now Jesse's standing outside the door to Room A23, feeling like nothing could be worse than missing the beginning of this meeting and having to barge in with Esther after it's already underway. Maybe she should just go inside and wait for Esther there. But Emily is almost certainly in there already, and the only fate worse than having to barge in disruptively with Esther is having to walk into that room, and come face-to-face with Emily, who has no idea she's about to see her, alone.

Because despite herself, despite the fear of exposure and the seriousness of her mission and the strong possibility that something disastrous is about to go down, knowing that Emily is so close right now fills Jesse with desire. Bold, uncontrollable desire, so that over and over again Jesse imagines flinging open the door to A23 and striding across the room to wherever Emily is sitting and grabbing her by the hand, hauling her to her feet, and dragging her out into the hall to kiss her. Again and again she imagines it: the shock on the faces of the other student council members, Emily's stunned acquiescence, her stumbling along behind Jesse into the hall, the sweet feeling of her arms looping around Jesse's neck as Jesse pushes her back against the lockers and—

"Hey!" At last Esther trundles around the corner, open book in one hand by her side, tote thumping against her other side. Jesse hisses, "Hurry!" and beckons her with big circles, like a third-base coach waving a runner home. "You're late!"

"I was reading," Esther says simply.

Inside A23 the meeting hasn't officially started, but the room is crowded and noisy with chatter. The desks have been configured in a big U shape, and the twelve members of student council are already seated at them, facing in. A bunch of other chairs have been set out in rows facing the desks, and ten or twelve kids are sitting there in the audience. Everybody is urgently talking to everybody else.

Jesse's eyes find Emily without even trying. She's presiding over the U, seated right in the center, with a bunch of file folders and an open notebook spread out in front of her, and she's leaning over to talk to Melissa Formosa, the pointy-nosed student council president. When she meets Jesse's eye she stops talking mid-sentence. Her mouth hangs open, and she drifts away from Melissa, slowly sitting up straight in her chair. Melissa turns to follow Emily's gaze and looks confusedly at Jesse, then back at

Emily. Automatically, Jesse drops her eyes to the floor.

"Over here," Esther says, tugging Jesse by the sleeve to a pair of chairs in the last row of the audience section, directly under the old pull-down map of Europe that still shows the Soviet Union, big, pink, and sprawling. Before they've even sat down, Melissa is ineffectually calling the meeting to order.

"Okay?" she pleads in her hollow, nasal voice. "Okay, people? We need to start, please?"

Slowly, the chatter dies down.

"Thanks, you guys," Melissa whines. "Thanks for listening up. Okay, so we have a lot to get through today, right, Emily?"

Emily nods, focusing fiercely on the papers in front of her. Jesse can feel Emily *not* looking at her as intensely as she would feel her looking at her.

"Will you tell us what's first on the agenda, Emily?"

Emily looks up and addresses the room with a careful, assembled smile. "Hi, everyone. Our first action item today is the establishment of a spirit banner committee for the lacrosse tournament at the end of the month. It's an away tournament, and we need volunteers to come to Maggie or Grace's house this weekend and help get banners ready that can travel with the team on the bus."

In the front row of the audience, a kid with shoulder-length blond curls sticking out from under his striped ski hat raises his hand high.

"We're not taking comments from the audience yet," Emily says briskly, barely looking at him.

"Yeah, I have a question about the flyers that were posted?" he asks anyway.

"We'll take questions once we've proceeded through all our action items. There are actually thirteen items on the agenda today, so it might take a little while."

Even in this dumb environment, even in the middle of a U of dumb student council members, even saying dumb things like *action items*, Emily is so, so beautiful to Jesse. She's pearly and golden and rosebud pink. Her cheeks are painfully soft, and her glossy hair—she's wearing it down today—is just begging to be touched. Her long, kissable neck draws Jesse's eye along it, the way it curves down, down, down all the way from her jawline into the crisp, white V of her open collar—

"Can we, like, talk about the flyers before you talk about the other stuff on your list?" the curly-hat kid asks, and a bunch of other kids in the audience back him up.

Emily turns to Melissa sharply. "Melissa, are we allowed to deviate from the agenda?" she asks. It's such a transparent move—clearly she's issuing a command, but disguising it as a query from a subordinate to a president.

"Maybe, actually, today we should?" Melissa ventures cautiously, but Emily jumps right on this.

"No, we can't deviate from the agenda or we might never get all the issues on the list addressed," she insists, her voice bright and brittle now. "The list has been planned for over three days. We have an obligation to deal with all these items."

Jesse has never seen Emily this close to losing her cool. And she's seen her in some pretty compromising positions.

"But people really want to talk about the flyers," Melissa tries again, timidly.

"Maybe we should put it to a vote." Emily sweeps her gaze over her fellow council members. "Council?"

"I think we totally need to talk about the StarMart thing," a girl with chunky hipster glasses and a blunt, black bob says, and rapidly the rest of the council agrees.

"Yeah, I think this is actually a major problem," the skinny guy in a rugby shirt seated on Emily's left says.

"I had no idea we were even taking money from them," says the tall girl at the end of the U of desks.

Emily glares down into her binder. Jesse sees that, very slightly, she's trembling.

"All right," Emily says after a beat. "All right, let's revise the agenda so the NorthStar support question is now the first action item on the list." She makes a couple of sharp notes on the paper in front of her.

"Comments from the student body?" Melissa Formosa asks, and though Emily gives her a reproachful look, hands go up all around the room.

"Yeah, are, like, the flyers true?" Curly-Hat asks.

"What about them?" Emily shoots back.

"Well, like, is it true that our school is being taken over by StarMart?"

"Our school is not being taken over by StarMart," Emily asserts firmly.

Beside Jesse, Esther stands up.

"Everything on the flyers is true," Esther declares with a certain grandness. Jesse feels her cheeks flush. The whole room turns to look at Esther.

"Excuse me, can you please raise your hand to be recognized by the council before you speak?" Emily asks crisply. The edges of her words are razor sharp.

Esther raises her right hand perfunctorily, as if she's being sworn in on a witness stand, and keeps talking. "The students of Vander High School need to know the truth about StarMart."

"Are you the one behind those flyers?" Emily asks Esther.

"Yes, along with my—"

"Well, I'm actually really glad you're here this afternoon, so you can see firsthand how much damage they've already caused."

"Damage?" Esther asks. "How can the truth cause damage?"

"Well," Emily explains hyper-calmly, just this side of condescendingly, "right now the posters are damaging the student council's effort to build connections with our larger community. This is something student council has been working really hard on for a couple of months now, and NorthStar is a really important connection we've made, a really important potential resource for Vander, and it's going to be really damaging to us if people start interfering in our relationship with NorthStar based on false or misleading information."

"There's nothing false on the flyer." Jesse feels herself stand up, hears herself speak. Her awareness is a beat behind her actions, so that she only realizes that she's on her feet when Emily turns to look at her.

Emily's eyes narrow slightly.

"Are you working with her?" Emily asks Jesse. The question is abrupt—too emotional, too personal—and it hangs oddly in the air between them, out of place in the public forum of Room A23.

When Jesse meets Emily's eye, she feels her voice drop away—down, down, down until it lands, far out of reach, at the bottom of her throat.

"We're partners," Esther says in the space left by Jesse's silence. Jesse sees a quick ripple of something—fear? resentment? rage?—pass through Emily's otherwise calm face.

"So, like, where did you guys get the information on the flyers?" Black-Haired-Bob Girl asks Esther and Jesse directly.

Esther explains. "It's easy to find out about StarMart and the things they do when they move into a new town.

It's all really well documented. You can look on the Internet, like on sprawlwatch.net or many other different sites about—"

"The *Internet*," Emily interrupts. "Everybody knows you can't trust what you read on the Internet."

"The statistics about local businesses are from an article in *The New York Times*," Esther continues. "The stuff about sweatshops comes from Amnesty International. We brought a bibliography of our sources to pass around." Esther addresses this to Jesse, prompting her, and somehow it breaks the silence spell Emily had cast over her. Her voice surges back into her throat again.

"Yeah, I have flyers." Jesse reaches into her bag and pulls out the ream of pink photocopies she brought with her. Her voice grows stronger as she speaks. "If you go to the website we have on here, you can sign our online petition. We believe that, as a public school, we shouldn't be taking money from private corporations, especially ones that are in, like, disputes with our town government. You guys should seriously all sign the petition. And forward it to your friends."

"What was the address for that? Can you read it out?" Black-Haired-Bob Girl asks, her pen poised.

Jesse opens her mouth to give the web address, but at that moment Emily catches her eye.

The look Emily gives Jesse is baffled and betrayed. She seems to ask, silently, *Why would you do this to me?*

In this second, Jesse feels the space between them collapse; she's transported to the bathroom in the library, transported to a place where there is no distance between her body and Emily's, where they are in perfect alignment, where they know each other extremely well and love each other exactly right. She's transported, briefly, into the center of a perfect kiss.

"Sprawlwatch dot net," Esther supplies, since Jesse's voice seems to have vanished again.

"Yeah," Jesse says hoarsely. She breaks Emily's gaze to look at Esther. "Sprawlwatch dot net."

✻ ✻ ✻

When Jesse comes stumbling out of the student council meeting, she is filled with more vibrant, swirling mixed feelings than she's ever felt at one time before. Esther is ecstatic beside her, practically crowing with glee.

"All of them," Esther giggles breathlessly. "Every single one of those kids is signing that petition right now! You know they are."

"They were totally into it," Jesse agrees.

It's a gorgeous afternoon, chilly and bright, with red, orange, and gold leaves fluttering hot against the blue sky all around them—the kind of crisp, high-definition fall weather Jesse loves. But her insides are a muddled blur.

Esther's right: every single one of those kids is busy forwarding that petition to their friends right now. Moments ago, when Esther and Jesse walked out of A23, every other kid who was not on student council went with them. No one had come to that meeting to make banners for the lacrosse tournament or figure out clever new ways to get kids to sell more fund-raising chocolate. Everyone was there to talk about getting StarMart out of Vander NOW!

Everyone except Emily. In the end she shut down debate before it was even over—there were still kids who wanted to ask questions when Emily forced them all to move on to the next "action item," or whatever she called it. She interrupted Esther in the middle of a sentence. She insulted their flyers. Jesse can't even imagine what's going to happen in the handicapped bathroom next Tuesday afternoon.

"Hey," Esther says, "let's go get cocoa at Beverly Coffee! Don't you want to? I feel like a giant hot cocoa with whipped cream and shaved chocolate right now." She slips her arm companionably through the crook of Jesse's elbow, and snugs Jesse close in a friendly squeeze.

"Yeah," Jesse says. "That sounds perfect."

Just then Jesse sees, from across the school's wide front lawn, Wyatt stand up from the bench where he's been sitting. Has he been waiting there for her since before school got out? Was she supposed to meet up with him today?

As he walks toward them, he calls out, "Howdy," in

a relaxed voice. He's still too far away for Jesse to tell whether he's mad or not.

"Hi!" she calls back, and gently disengages her arm from Esther's. She uses it to wave at Wyatt once it's free, as if to justify to Esther why she pulled away.

As Wyatt gets closer, Jesse can see that his Western wear is in full swing now; under his navy-blue windbreaker, it appears he is wearing fringed chaps.

"This is Esther," Jesse almost shouts, too loud and too soon. There's no reason for her to be yelling this introduction across such a distance, except that she's somehow nervous to be making it and wants to get it over with soon.

Wyatt keeps walking toward them, unhurried. "Wyatt Willette," he says when he's reached hand-shaking distance. He takes Esther's hand in his.

"This is Esther," Jesse says again, gesturing redundantly. "She's a ninth-grader. Esther, this is Wyatt. He's homeschooled."

"That's an activity, not an identity," Wyatt explains suavely.

"Nice to meet you." Esther shakes Wyatt's hand with tons of energy and no grace whatsoever. When she releases it, Jesse catches Wyatt looking down to inspect his open palm, as if Esther had altered it somehow by shaking it.

"So what kept you kids so long?" Wyatt looks Jesse over, assessing her coolly. "I thought I would catch you on your way out of school. Too bad about your phone being broken."

"My phone's not—" Jesse starts, then bites her lip. "Sorry."

"Yeah, I thought after eight messages I should just come find you. Make sure you were still alive."

Jesse looks down at the ground.

"We were just fighting for justice in there!" Esther exults, and laughs her strange little bark-whoop laugh.

Wyatt raises his eyebrows archly. "Fighting for justice? Inside the halls of Vander High? I find that hard to believe."

"Oh, it's true! You should have seen us. We brought the student council to its *knees* just now."

"Really? Student council?" Wyatt purrs, smooth as a milk shake. "Well, that's like slaying a dragon, isn't it? That's news. I expect to read about that in *The New York Times* tomorrow morning."

"Wyatt—" Jesse begins, but Esther laughs, undeterred.

"Yeah, okay, that might seem like small potatoes to you, but how do you think big things get done? One little bit at a time, right? Hey, Jesse and I are going to Beverly Coffee to get some cocoa, do you want to come with us?"

Wyatt meets Jesse's eye for a moment.

"Oh," he says, careful and polite, "I do appreciate the offer, but I'm afraid I have to visit local thrifting establishment Rose's Turn this afternoon. I thought my friend Jesse might join me, as she often has in the past. But I see you two have plans. That's fine. I don't want to intrude."

"You wouldn't be intruding," Esther insists.

"No, come with us. Please come with us?" Jesse urges him.

Wyatt squints at Jesse for a second now. "It's tempting," he says, "but I'm on the verge of a breakthrough with my new Charles Lindbergh look, and I don't think I can wait another day to find the right aviator scarf. Plus, I don't want to miss Marla's shift. Last time I was there she gave me a free pair of tassel loafers. You girls have fun."

Wyatt turns and begins walking away, down the access road that leads in the opposite direction from town. And in the opposite direction from Rose's Turn, Jesse realizes.

She calls after him, "I'll totally come with you next week!"

Without turning around, Wyatt lifts his hand to wave.

13

Emily

I couldn't wait for next Tuesday—almost an entire week—to talk to Jesse about what she did. I felt like her showing up to my meeting was the beginning of something very, very bad, and I could tell that if I didn't nip it in the bud, it would be out of control in only a few seconds. So I emailed her—the first time I had ever used the email address she gave me almost a year ago, actually—and asked her if we could move our regular meeting up from Tuesday to Friday afternoon. She emailed back one word: "Okay."

I told my mom that I had to check in with Carol at the library about something on the way home and that's why I'd be late to help with dinner on Friday. She was fine about it. She's very big on honoring your commitments and showing the people who put their trust in you by hiring you that you're responsible (partly because at her job as office manager of the Dower Group she's always having to cover for people who don't pull their own weight, so she really disapproves of slacking off of any kind). As soon as school was over on Friday, I went straight to the library, straight through the back entrance, and straight up the back stairs to the handicapped restroom on the third floor. Jesse didn't get there until 3:05, so I had almost twenty-five minutes to gather my thoughts and prepare for exactly how I wanted to talk to her. I was more than ready to have the conversation I wanted to have with her by the time she knocked on the door.

I started out totally reasonable and calm. I was like, Hey, I just wanted to talk to you for a second about what happened at that meeting, and I know we're probably going to disagree about some things, but—

Right away she cut me off. She was like, Yeah, we are. All snappish. I could see that she was totally upset.

I could have stopped then or changed direction. I could have tried to calm her down or lied to her about how I felt, but I really wanted us to have an honest conversation, so I was like, Look, we don't have to talk about the things you said about NorthStar, which I don't happen to agree with, but—

And she cut me off again. She was like, It's not a question of you *agreeing* with me or not, the facts are the facts.

I took a deep breath, like my mom always says to do whenever you find yourself in an escalating situation. I reminded myself that all I had to do was get her to see my side of things. I didn't need to make her change her crazy mind.

So I was like, Okay, whatever, the thing that I need you to know right now is that the NorthStar project is actually my baby, it's really, really important to me, and I need you to not keep going with this campaign to get rid of them because it's seriously messing up all my plans.

She looked at me sort of funny then, and she was like, What do you mean, your "baby"?

I explained my whole history with NorthStar, I was like, This is actually an idea I came up with on my own, I approached NorthStar personally and I made it happen and I'm working with them at their office once a week. I was like, It's okay, I know you didn't know that because I didn't tell you but it's actually been an incredible experience so far and also it's a really big deal for Vander and you just need to please back off on this one. For me.

Jesse was weirdly quiet then—kind of scary quiet.

She was like, You're *working* with them?

I was like, Yeah. I told her about the unpaid internship and the office and the giant copier and how nice everyone is to me over there—all the things I wished I could have told her before—and she just kept getting weirder and weirder, quieter and quieter. I was like, Please don't freak out, I know this is not something you would probably do but we just have to agree to disagree about this. And then I said the thing I had been planning to say all along, I was like, Working with NorthStar is just as important to me as your poster things are to you, so I really wish you would respect that and stop doing this right now. I'm not saying stop doing posters altogether, I'm just saying could you please go back to doing posters that are random, like before, where they didn't actually have any effect on people or cause any damage, instead of using them to try to destroy my life like you are now?

Jesse was like, My posters have never been random. Like, *super* pissed. She was all, Did you even look at the StarMart posters? Did you look at the flyers we handed out at your meeting? Everything on them is real. How can you keep working for them when you know all the horrible things they do? StarMart is the enemy.

So I was like, That is so crazy, they are not the *enemy*, you might not agree with everything they do, but they actually do lots of amazing things for the world that you don't even know about.

She was like, Esther says they're the single-most evil corporation in the world.

I was like, Esther? Is she that girl you were with at the meeting? Do you like her or something?

And Jesse was like, No.

I was like, Is she your new girlfriend?

And she was like, No!

But she didn't look at me when she said it.

I'm pretty comfortable being in competitive situations. I like to work hard, and I like to earn what I get. But I guess I sort of always assumed that I wouldn't have to be in a competitive situation when it came to Jesse. The thing about being with Jesse that's been so incredible for me since the beginning is that because we're so different, because we barely agree on anything, I've always been able to feel how pure our feelings for each other are. It's not like there's any public part of our relationship, like with me and Michael, where other people want us to stay together, and it's not like we agree with each other's ideas or enjoy talking about things or have anything in common or anything. It's deeper than that. It's a soul connection. And I guess that's why I never thought I would have to compete for Jesse's attention.

Not that I have any objection to that girl she was with at the meeting, I'm sure she has a really great personality and she's probably good in school, which are both things I'm sure Jesse cares about a lot. She is a little weird looking, to be totally honest—those messy Heidi braids? those long old-lady skirts?—but she's no weirder than Jesse is. I guess I just thought that wasn't the kind of girl Jesse was interested in.

I was thinking about this, about the kind of girls Jesse likes, when Jesse launched into this huge rant about NorthStar. She used to do this more before she realized that I'm basically immune to her insanity. And I have to say, as boring and annoying as it was when she used to rant about stuff that was hardly even real, like nuclear war or famine or whatever, this was so much worse. Listening to her rant about NorthStar, which she doesn't even *know* anything about and which is part of our actual *lives*, just made me more and more and more angry. She was, like, thlomping back and forth across the bathroom in her hobo boots, going on and on about all the supposedly terrible things NorthStar does, and how they're trying to take over the world, and asking me, like, don't I care about workers in Honduras blah blah blah and don't I care about protecting local stores blah blah and don't I care about the poor little kids of StarMart employees who can't even afford to go the doctor blah blah blabbedy blah and finally I was like, Stop, stop, *stop!*

I was practically yelling at her—we were both practically yelling. We both totally forgot about staying quiet in our private place. I was like, None of that has anything to do with me! Even if some of that stuff is true about North-Star, it's totally beside the point! The point is I'm trying to do something good for our school, which will benefit everybody at Vander, *including you!*

Then Jesse stopped pacing, and came over and stood really close to me and clamped her hands on my upper arms like she sometimes does, sort of holding me in place, and she looked deep into my eyes with that really intense laser-beam gaze she has, where it feels like she's looking right through your body into a deeper space, right into the center of your private soul. I can remember every single time in my life Jesse has looked at me like that. Each time it's been right before she's touched me or kissed me so intensely that I've basically temporarily lost my mind. Each time it's been right before she got closer to me than any other human being has ever been.

She looked into my eyes like that, and I felt my stomach flip. My eyes closed. I was so ready for her. I was so ready for our fight to be over. I thought, *Finally, she's going to see my side. As soon as she kisses me, it'll all be done.*

She was so close to me I felt the warmth of her breath on my face when she spoke. She did not kiss me. Instead she said very quietly, Do you even have a conscience, Emily? Do you even have a heart?

It was the first time I ever heard her say my name.

I opened my eyes but I didn't recognize her. She was four inches away from me—so close—and she looked like a total stranger. The features of her face were off-kilter and odd. Her face didn't even look like a human face to me.

I felt super scared. I felt super alone.

I realized then that I was going to cry. It was so sudden and so incredible to me. I didn't plan it. I just, like, felt the tears move up into position, felt that wavery feeling take over inside my chest, and then I was crying and crying and crying. It seemed like I was crying a year's worth of tears. Once I started, I felt like I was never going to be able to stop. I felt like I was melting inside. I felt like I was falling down, down, down, and no one was ever going to be able to catch me. I covered my face with my hands and cried.

Then I felt Jesse put her arms around me.

Not looking at her, just feeling her hold me, I recognized her again. This was the Jesse I knew, the holding Jesse, the strong and quiet Jesse, the sweet-smelling Jesse who knows me so well, who makes me feel better in that one particular way than anyone else in the entire world.

After the crying wound down and I got myself together again I went back to the conversation I had planned to have. I told her, point-blank, to please please *please* choose something else to protest. I told her that I know she always needs to have a cause or whatever, but couldn't she please go save baby seals or help illegal immigrants become citizens or something? Anything, anything other than this? I kept my arms around her while I said it, so she couldn't break free from me and start ranting again. And I tried to reassure her that NorthStar is actually a really good company with strong values and an incredible mission. I told her that she's seriously overreacting when she talks about them trying to take over the world.

I could feel her trying to figure out what to do. She was looking up at the ceiling and down at the floor and out the little frosted window above the sink but not at me, not *at* me. So I kissed her. I put my hands on her head like she always puts her hands on mine, and I turned her face to me and I kissed her. Thank God she kissed me back. It felt incredible. It was such a relief, like taking a first deep breath of air after being underwater for too long.

We had a sort of scary-intense time after that. She was so . . . I don't know, she was so hungry and bold. Somehow, at some point, she got my shirt all the way off. I let my shirt go, and then I let myself go. I gave in to her completely.

Something amazing happened between us then— something deeper, and different from everything that came before. She didn't say it to me out loud, but I know she's going to drop the NorthStar protest. She has to. We've both made sacrifices for each other now, and I feel more bonded to her than ever.

But I also feel like I have to be more careful from now on about how I interact with her, and how often. When I was walking home, more than an hour late to help my mom, I started to think that maybe we should take a little break from seeing each other, just for a while, just until we both cool down a little. When she was kissing me this time . . . I don't know how to explain it. She was so aggressive. She bit me all over a little, hard and sharp. Like she was trying to leave marks.

14

Jesse

First period on Monday morning, and Jesse is clutching the smooth wooden bathroom pass in her right hand. She hovers in the drinking-fountain alcove by the sophomore hall girls' room, waiting for a pair of girls to clear out of there so she can go in and sweep the room for the last traces of the anti-StarMart campaign. Most of the yellow posters have already been taken down by teachers and custodians, the ones in the high-traffic areas: bulletin boards and fire doors and hallways. And of course, the campaign has already done what it was supposed to do: people can't un-see what they've seen, un-talk-about what they've talked about. But for Emily's sake, Jesse has decided to eradicate every last remnant of the poster campaign, the ones she knows are still up in nooks and crannies around the school: girls' rooms, mostly, and out-of-the-way, high-up places where even custodians don't think—or don't bother—to look. The pockets of her cargo pants and the front pouch of her backpack are already full of crumpled goldenrod-yellow paper.

She spent the past weekend in self-imposed isolation, ignoring phone calls from Esther and trying to keep her eyes closed as much as possible so she could stay in the memory of Emily in the bathroom on Friday afternoon. The feel of her skin against Jesse's own, the explosion of softness and intensity, like an underground nuclear bomb test. . . . Jesse felt her loyalties melt away completely the moment she pulled Emily's shirt off over her head. She felt ravenous, half blind with hunger, like an animal. When they left the bathroom, neither one of them could look the other one in the eye. And the aftershocks kept moving through Jesse all weekend. Esther called twice on Saturday to ask if Jesse was coming to the vigil again or not, but Jesse let the calls go to voice mail and didn't call back. This morning on her way in to school, she was careful to avoid the freshman hall and head straight to homeroom, so she wouldn't have to see Esther and explain herself to her.

The two girls leave the bathroom at last, and Jesse slips in. There are four posters still on the wall in here, high above the bank of mirrors over the sinks. Apparently, it was easy enough to tape them up there in the first place—she must have leapt up onto the sinks like Superman and sailed back down: No fear. Was Esther with her in this bathroom, spotting her when she climbed up, tearing off pieces of tape and passing them to her? How can Jesse not remember what it was like to post these, which she herself personally did, only a few days ago? She was in a haze of purpose then. Only the plan existed, and the partnership between her and Esther—the logistical details were nothing to them, tiny hurdles they sailed over on wings of enthusiasm.

Now she's wingless. Land-bound, with two left feet inside a pair of boots that couldn't be more wrong for this operation. She feels unprepared, out of balance. As she starts to hoist herself up onto the sink, she catches her own reflection in the mirror.

She doesn't look like much. Dark, empty eyes. Backpack hanging, lopsided, off her shoulders. Ringer tee, cargo pants, and a suddenly girly haircut. Overnight, her hair has gone from just right to way too long. It does this— puffs up from badass to embarrassing over the course of what seems like a matter of hours. She needs to take her Swiss Army Knife to it as soon as she gets the chance. When she gazes back at herself from the mirror she looks shaggy and lost.

Jesse scrambles awkwardly to her feet on the sink, but she's wobbly in the boots, unsteady on the wet, slippery porcelain. She clutches desperately at the mirror's narrow edge as she reaches for the first bright-yellow poster. When the burst of static comes from right outside the door, she's about as hidden as a target at a shooting range.

Jesse freezes mid-reach. She closes her eyes and feels the slight breeze move around her as the door creaks open. She senses more than sees Snediker's squat, compact body anchored in the door frame down to her left.

"Well, well, well," Snediker whines. "This is getting to be kind of a habit with you."

Jesse swallows, and looks down at her. From this vantage point, with Snediker so short and Jesse up so high, the dean of students looks like a peevish elf. Her round, rosy face is placid, as always, under the tight cap of her perm. She props her small, balled fists up on either side of her belly. When she moves her arms, the ring of warden-keys she keeps bungee-corded around her wrist jingles.

"I was trying to take it down," Jesse says dumbly. She hasn't moved since the door opened; her arm is still stretched over her head, reaching. Her big green boots are still propped wide on either side of the sink.

Snediker smiles her miserly smile, her lips drawn into a short, straight line. "I'm afraid that's neither here nor there." The walkie-talkie clipped to her blazer pocket emits a staticky crackle. A voice on it says, "We have a situation in four ten, situation in four ten, over."

"Come on down," Snediker says, a chillingly friendly invitation. She beckons to Jesse. "You're coming with me."

THE DIFFERENCE BETWEEN **YOU** AND **ME**

* * *

Snediker makes Jesse wait for some time in the row of red chairs lining the narrow hallway outside her office.

"Ms. Yost is probably waiting for her pass . . . ?" Jesse suggests when Snediker seats her there, holding up the bathroom pass in question.

"Ms. Yost knows where her pass is." Snediker passes Jesses calmly, without looking at her. She goes into her office and shuts the door.

The last time Jesse was remanded here, she only made it as far as the outside reception area. The inner sanctum, where she is now, is reserved for more serious offenders— Jesse has never been this far in before. She peers at the closed, featureless office door. Maybe Snediker actually does have something to do in there, or maybe this is just her tactic to get kids worked up into a frenzy of fear before she brings them in to skin, fillet, and fry them in oil.

Jesse waits.

It's the opposite of the peace vigil. The longer Jesse stood still at the vigil, the more it felt right, and alive, and real. The more she felt like she was putting her body where her beliefs were. And she noticed more and more things about the world around her, too, the longer she stood there with Esther, Margaret, Charlie, and Arlo. The exact blue of the sky, the exact grain of the bark on the tree near the exact Ford Taurus parked near the exact toothpaste-green parking meter . . . the exact stride of Mike McDade striding down the sidewalk to the exact door with the exact bell of Murray and Sons Hardware.

Now the details of the world around her are blurring, not sharpening. She sees less and less, hears less and less, sinks deeper and deeper into the murky tide of disgust and disappointment—mixed with a little bubbly water of fear—that's rising up through her, taking over her whole midsection, the breathing and digesting parts of her body, making her feel like she's drowning inside herself. What could Snediker have in store for her this time? If she went straight to ASP for the spirit-assembly window-leap, what will the sentence be for her second offense? Out-of-school suspension? For a week? For a month? And a big black mark on her permanent record that will ruin her chances of *ever* getting into NYU?

When Jesse thinks of what her mother's going to do when she hears about this . . . she *can't* think about what her mother's going to do when she hears about this.

In a burst of self-recrimination, Jesse thinks, *See,* this *is why Emily is with Mike!* Obviously, Mike McDade would never do something like this. Obviously, he would never dream of undermining his girlfriend's student council project. And more than that, he would never be so idiotic as to be caught trying to take back something he had already irrevocably done. He would never be so inconsistent, so sloppy, so dumb. He would never end up outside Snediker's office, waiting to be dragged in to answer for his own stupid actions. Mike McDade is a solid citizen. And Emily is, too.

The door swings open, and Jesse looks up. Snediker is all the way across the wood-paneled room, perched behind her metal desk. With what dark art did she make the door open from so far away?

"I'm ready for you now," Snediker says tonelessly, and Jesse rises.

The chair of the condemned, opposite the desk, is intentionally hard and straight-backed. When Jesse sits in it she immediately feels the seat bore into her butt in two knobbly places. Does Snediker have special butt-boring panels installed in her punishment chair? It's possible.

Snediker settles a little in her seat. Above her on the wall hangs a huge, framed painting of autumn trees fringing the edge of a rippling blue lake. In front of her, the desk is bare except for her computer monitor and keyboard, placed at an angle to her seat; a white mug filled with identical black-capped ball-point pens; and an ancient push-button phone the color of an Ace bandage.

"I haven't called your folks yet," Snediker begins, and Jesse experiences a surge of relief so strong she has to hold herself back from weeping. She nods vigorously. "But I will when we're done talking." The relief drains away, and Jesse nods again listlessly. From a drawer in the right-hand side of her desk, Snediker produces a manila folder, which she opens casually in front of her. It's full of brightly colored papers—familiar to Jesse from a year's worth of manifesto work—which she pages through as she speaks.

"Destruction of school property," Snediker intones, and flips a neon-orange paper over facedown on the desk. Jesse recognizes it as her first-ever manifesto. "Destruction of school property." Snediker flips an emerald-green paper over—Jesse's second opus. "Vandalism." Cherry-red paper—flip. "Destruction of school property." Sky-blue paper—flip. "Destruction of school property and misuse of hall pass." She holds this last paper—bright golden-rod yellow—up for Jesse to inspect. WAKE UP, VANDER! it reads across the top in 46-point font. SERIOUSLY!

Jesse bites her lip. "I was trying to take that one *down*," she explains again, but when she hears herself say this it sounds like such a feeble excuse that she wishes she had just kept her mouth shut.

"You've accumulated quite an evidence file here over the past year," Snediker observes. "What do you want to tell me about it?"

Jesse opens her mouth. What does she want to tell glassy-eyed, monotonous Dean Snediker about her manifestos? About her passion, her life's work, her best way of expressing herself, the thing that first brought her into contact with Esther, the thing that has ruined her love life and damaged her closest friendship and forced her to make up a series of pitifully stupid lies to explain to her mother why she kept burning through her toner? There's nothing she wants to tell Snediker about her manifestos. She shrugs.

"How do you know those are all mine?"

"Don't waste my time," Snediker says curtly. Jesse looks down, chastened. "Here's what I want to say to you about this file. A friendly warning from me to you. You might think these are a funny joke, but this kind of activity can land you in very hot water."

"I don't think they're a funny joke," Jesse manages quietly.

"You might think a little tape on a couple of walls is a trivial matter, but destruction of school property is not a trivial matter. It is a serious matter. Do you understand that this is a serious matter?"

Jesse looks at Snediker directly now. Her pink face is a creepy old-young combination, like an aging baby doll. Her blinkless, light blue eyes rest on Jesse without quite seeming to take her in.

"But people tape posters to the walls all the time," Jesse objects. "Every day people tape things up about, like, SADD meetings and bake sales and auditions for *The Pajama Game* or whatever."

"Those are school-related posters."

"This is school related!" Jesse cries, pointing to the StarMart poster. "This is totally about the school and what's happening to it without our permission!" She feels the righteous rage that has been so hard to tap into these past few days come surging back up to fill her again, warm and familiar.

"It's unofficial."

"Okay, so, so, wait, so a poster raising awareness about the corruption of the school by an outside corporation is unofficial, but a poster announcing a bake sale for Future Business Leaders of America is official?"

"Correct."

"So if I had an official school-sponsored group, I could put up any poster I wanted, talking about anything I wanted to talk about, but if I'm just one person without official status I can't put up any posters talking about anything at all?"

"No one has carte blanche to put up whatever flyers they want to around the school. Even official posters must follow certain rules."

"But I have a first-amendment right to free speech." This is Jesse's trump card and she delivers it grandly, but Snediker shakes her head impassively. Her dense bosom rides a wave of breath—up, then down—as she sighs.

"Your mistake, Ms. Halberstam," Snediker says, "is in believing that a school is a democracy. A school is not a democracy. It is not a country, so it cannot be a *free* country. This school is a benevolent dictatorship, and I am its leader."

"But, but what about Mr. Greil?" Jesse demands, sputtery. Doesn't the principal run the school?

"Mr. Greil is in charge of your learning, but I am in charge of your behavior. And the behaviors associated with your postering campaigns are unacceptable." Snediker ticks them off on her plump fingers. "Skipping class. Abusing hall passes. Damaging the paint job that Mr. Hubert and his crew spent so much time and effort refreshing over the summer. And quite frankly, disrupting the normal functioning of the school. Since this current campaign of yours began, I've gotten several quite threatening calls from parents and members of the community accusing Vander of selling its soul. One unhinged gentleman told me on the phone yesterday that I was personally 'colluding with the military-industrial complex.' Obviously, these accusations are groundless, but they're unhelpful, particularly right now in the middle of budget review season. You don't know what budget review season is, but it is in fact an important part of the school year that makes it possible for us to keep our doors open so that you and your fellow students can come here, study, learn, graduate, and go on to lead fulfilling lives. You should consider that there might be lots of other things you don't know about that keep this school going, things you throw into jeopardy when you make unfounded claims like these." Snediker pinches the yellow poster by its corner and holds it up again, a distasteful specimen.

"But they're not unfounded." Jesse has inherited Fran's dominant cross-examination gene; even though she spent the weekend renouncing the fight against StarMart, she can't let Snediker's misuse of the word *unfounded* go by without arguing it. "All the stuff on that poster is true. We did bunches of research on StarMart. And if that one poster, like, throws the school into jeopardy, maybe that's a risk we have to take. Maybe it's worth throwing some things into jeopardy to keep our school from being connected to an evil corporation." On the word *worth*, Jesse feels herself make Fran's signature power gesture—a chopping motion against the desk—with her right hand.

"I would be careful how I threw around the word *evil*, if I were you," Snediker reproaches her. "But I do . . . I do . . ." Snediker blinks now, and blinks again. Her eyelashes flutter unsettlingly for a moment, as if her inner workings have hit a glitch. Then she recalibrates, regains her evenness. "In principle, I understand the points you're trying to make here about StarMart. I may even agree with some of them. There was a time in my life when I might have been tempted to put up a couple of posters myself on behalf of a cause like this. But Jesse, I can't allow you to plaster your personal opinions all over school in this way. Especially if you excuse yourself from class to do it."

Jesse squints. Did Snediker just say she agrees with her?

"Listen. Some friendly advice from me to you. Have you ever heard the expression 'Pick your battles'?"

"Um . . . yes?"

"All right. You need to pick your battles right now. You may think you've got some kind of David and Goliath thing going on with StarMart, but I can guarantee you, this is a losing proposition. You're not going to change the way StarMart operates. They are an extremely powerful multinational corporation, and you're deluding yourself if you think that you and a couple of friends and a roll of tape can succeed in changing their global business model. What you *will* succeed in doing, if you continue to pursue this, is damaging school property, creating unrest and un-happiness in the student body, upsetting the community, and throwing your own future into jeopardy by making decisions that have negative disciplinary consequences. I won't hesitate to suspend you, or worse, if you continue to violate school rules. I will throw the book at you, Jesse. And I wouldn't like to see you permanently limit your life options by making reckless choices. That would be a real shame. You have a lot of potential. When I look at you, in some ways I see a young me."

"What?" Jesse can't keep the appalled look off her face. To her horror, Snediker laughs, a tinkly, dry little laugh.

"Oh, you think I was always a dean of students? I have been some places and done some things that I'm sure you wouldn't believe if I told you about them." Snediker gets a brief, vivid look of mischief in her eyes—it skeeves Jesse out so much that she has to look away. "I learned the hard way that there's nothing waiting at the end of that road down but pain and futility. Take it from me: pick your battles. Don't be a hero. The flyering stops now."

Jesse doesn't nod, doesn't say anything. After a moment she asks, "Am I suspended or something?"

"I'm going to issue you a warning at this time, because I believe that you listened well during our conversation and you understand what I'm saying to you about consequences. I'll call your parents to let them know that we've talked. But that's all. You're done. Back to Ms. Yost."

Snediker dismisses Jesse with a single stiff wave of her hand. She picks up the receiver of her clunky phone as Jesse gets up to go.

"Yes," Jesse hears behind her as she heads for the door, "this is Janet Snediker calling for Frances Halberstam."

When Jesse opens the door to Snediker's office, Emily is *right* there, in the first red chair by the door, slender legs crossed in her light blue jeans, hands folded on the neat stack of folders resting on her lap. She looks up, sees Jesse, and gasps faintly. Jesse closes the door so abruptly it almost slams.

"Are you waiting for me?" Jesse says, her eyes wide. It can't be, of course Emily's not waiting for Jesse, but in a shimmering moment of hope Jesse sees it all in heart-breaking detail: somehow Emily heard that Jesse got busted taking down the last posters, and she was so touched by the gesture that she gave up her open period to sit in patient vigil outside this office door, waiting for the moment when Jesse would be released. Now she'll grab Jesse's hand and lead her to the parking lot and the two of them will jump into Emily's little blue Honda, and kiss and kiss, and drive over to get lattes from Beverly Coffee—

"I have a meeting with Dean Snediker," Emily whispers. She looks around her furtively. They're the only two in the hallway, but still she contracts away from Jesse, trying to put as much distance between them as she can without crawling out of her chair. "To talk about Starry Starry Night."

"Oh." Jesse nods. "Cool. Hey, I did it. I took them all down."

"Took all what down?" Emily keeps shooting little looks over Jesse's shoulder.

"The anti-StarMart posters. I went through the whole school and took the last of them down this morning."

"Oh."

"That's what I got busted doing." Jesse gestures with her thumb to Snediker's closed door, a little swagger in the move.

"Great." Emily nods briefly. "Thanks."

Jesse stands there a minute in the narrow hallway, considering Emily. In some ways, this is an even more public moment for her and Emily than the student council meeting. Any second now they could be caught here alone together. What if she grabbed Emily's hand just as Snediker was opening the door? What if she bent down to kiss Emily right as Ms. Ewing, the director of instruction, came around the corner to make a photocopy? What would Emily do? What would Jesse do? What would change in the world if this secret came out?

Tempting fate, Jesse leans in close to Emily to whisper in her ear. "I'll see you Tuesday."

The thrilling fruit-and-flower scent of Emily wafts over Jesse, intoxicating her. She closes her eyes and breathes deep, lets it suffuse her completely.

But Emily pulls back. "Actually . . . I don't . . ." Her voice is so low it's barely audible. "I don't know if I can come this Tuesday."

"Oh." Jesse straightens up. "Okay. The Tuesday after, then." But somehow she already knows what Emily's about to say next.

"I don't know, I feel like . . . I'm just so busy right now?" Emily's whisper is regretful but vague. "The dance is taking up so much of my time, and things are so crazy in my life . . . I feel like I've been spreading myself too thin, you know?"

"No." Jesse says this at full volume, and Emily shushes her silently, one delicate finger to her lips.

"I just . . ." Now Emily beckons Jesse closer. Jesse bends

down mechanically. The familiar smell of her moves over Jesse again, but sharper this time, tangier, like a cleaning product. "I think maybe we should take a little break, just until things get calmer for me."

"When will that be?"

"I don't know, but soon."

"Like a year from now?"

"Of course not."

"A month from now?"

"I don't know."

Jesse nods. It's too awful to keep asking questions.

"Soon, I promise." Emily smiles at Jesse then, sweetly, encouragingly. "I'll email you as soon as things get back to normal, and we can start up with our regular Tuesdays again." She reaches out and runs her fingertips along the neckline of Jesse's ringer tee.

In her chest, in her throat, Jesse's heart burns.

From inside Snediker's office comes a scraping noise, the sound of a chair being pushed back from a desk. Emily sits bolt upright in her seat. With the same hand that was just caressing Jesse, she pushes her firmly away.

"Please," she begs as Jesse staggers back a step. "Go. You can't be here when she calls me in."

15

Esther

The first difference between Joan and other saints—girl saints anyway—is that Joan *did* stuff. She took action.

Most girl saints are all about waiting, enduring, sacrificing. They live for twenty years in a stone cell eating only bread and water and contemplating God through a tiny window, or they quietly take care of lepers until they themselves die of leprosy, or they get tortured by heretics and never renounce their faith even while they're being disemboweled or whatever. Those things are awesome, I totally admire those things. Frankly, I would love to work with lepers someday. But what I love about Joan is that she *did* things. She made big decisions, and she made other people carry out her ideas. She didn't wait for permission. She just acted.

Her voices told her, "Get yourself to this neighboring village and dress up like a boy soldier"? She did it. Her voices told her, "Go inform the true king of France that

THE DIFFERENCE BETWEEN **YOU** AND **ME**

even though you've never been to battle or ridden a horse and you are a skinny seventeen-year-old girl, you are his new general"? Done. They said, "Liberate the city of Orléans, which has been under siege by the English for months and which no other armies have been able to free"? Boom: she did it. At so many moments along the way she could have been like, "Wait a second, this is a *terrible* idea. This is going to end in tears. I'm out." But she never did. She never stopped taking action.

The first night Joan slept in her new armor, it was so heavy and she was so small that she woke up covered in bruises. She looked her body over, splashed her face with water, got up on her horse, and rode toward battle.

When someone in your family gets sick, really sick, you spend a ton of time waiting, doing nothing. It starts to be your main family activity. You're always waiting in some salmon-colored vinyl chair under a fluorescent light, waiting in a line to fill out an intake form, waiting for your name to be called, waiting in the kitchen for your parents to get home, waiting a week for the results to come in. People are always telling you, "We're waiting for this screen to come back," or "We have to wait to schedule the next treatment until your levels go up." Meanwhile, all the time, the clock is ticking.

My mom was the patient. I was impatient. I wanted someone—anyone—to do something big.

In principle, I don't believe in war or violence in any

form. In that way, I'm not like Joan—I hardly ever get that kind of hot, bursting feeling in your chest that makes you want to grab a weapon and charge. But when my mother was being held prisoner in that hospital, at the end, and they were doing all those things to her that seemed like pure torture, I did fantasize all the time about blasting open the doors of the receiving area with a blowtorch, and marching down the halls with a machine gun and chains of ammunition strapped across my chest, picking her up out of that hospital bed, and carrying her out in my arms, through the automatic doors into the parking lot. Swinging her up over the back of my horse and riding off with her. Knocking down anyone who got in my way. It was pretty much the only time in my life when I ever wanted to commit a violent act. So I do know that I'm capable of it.

But I never did it, of course. Dr. Moench said, "We have to wait for six months after surgery before we consider a more aggressive course of treatment." And we all said, "Okay." Dr. Ratner said, "As soon as the histology report comes in, we'll know better what our options are." And we all said, "Okay." We weren't bold. We weren't demanding. We didn't want to risk making a mistake, and losing everything.

This is the second thing about Joan that makes her different from other saints. Because she got her instructions directly from saints and angels, and because she liked to do big things, she made, like, a ton of mistakes. Most girl saints don't make big mistakes because they don't have the chance to. They're, like, walled up in their cell or hanging out alone in their leper colony or whatever, not really bothering anybody. Joan made big mistakes, and in the end they had big, terrible consequences.

Not at first—at first she was a natural-born genius of war. She defied the wisdom of the older male generals and led her army straight into besieged Orléans, even though no army units had been able to liberate that city for over a year. When the generals were like, "You must wait," Joan didn't sit back in her salmon-covered vinyl chair and say, "Okay." She was like, "No more waiting. Now." Through a few brilliant, insanely bold moves, she beat back the English and Orléans was freed. Nobody could believe it. It was a miracle.

And for a while she rode the miracle. She won battle after battle, against all odds, and the hungry, hopeful peasants of France called her invincible. But eventually, she overreached. The numbers in her army dwindled, and she worked her men—and herself—so hard that they found themselves in over their heads. At Compiègne, Joan was captured mid-battle, and taken prisoner by the English.

When I was little, the one picture in my Joan book that I couldn't bear to look at showed Joan in the middle of her last battle, when she got shot in the shoulder and dragged down off her horse's back by the enemy. In this picture, her horse is writhing in pain, his lips and nostrils flaring, his eyes huge. His front legs are up and he's halfway through throwing Joan off his back. Joan's eyes are closed, her hand moving up toward where the arrow has embedded itself in her shoulder, and she's come a few inches up off her saddle. She's about to topple into the mud but she hasn't yet. Her blue standard is on its way down to the ground but hasn't yet hit. Joan is suspended, floating between glory and defeat.

I used to pinch those pages closed when I read the book to keep from having to see Joan fail. But now I love that picture. I love it so much. I love how Joan kept going right up to the end. It reminds me that sometimes defeat is the price of taking action. If you *do* something, you become a target. People want to take you down. That's a risk. But it's better to do too much, better to try too hard, better to have a crisis of faith and get thrown and climb back up on your horse and keep riding, than to see something wrong in the world and not do anything at all.

Anyway, if you need your heroes to be perfect, you won't have very many. Even Superman had his kryptonite. I'd rather have my heroes be more like me: Trying to do the right thing, sometimes messing up. Making mistakes. Saying they're sorry. And forgiving other people when they mess up, too.

16

Jesse

Jesse lies on the living room couch with the morning sun-light stalled over her, warming her afghan-covered legs. She's in her navy-blue cutoff sweatpants and white men's undershirt, and she has the props of illness arranged around her: TV on mute tuned to the Home Shopping Net-work (a woman's hands silently stroking a trio of fake dia-mond bracelets), Tylenol, and flat ginger ale with a bendy straw in it on the end table by her head. She managed to convince Arthur, if not Fran, that she was too unwell for school this morning, but she doesn't have a fever. Only her heart is sick.

Her parents are huddled outside the living room door right now, arguing in low, urgent voices. Since yesterday, when Jesse broke down sobbing during the confrontation that followed Snediker's phone call, both Fran and Arthur have given Jesse a wide berth. Her crying was so sudden, so unlike her, and so unstoppable that her parents uncharacteristically let Jesse retreat to her room before dinner without making her talk it all through.

Now that a night has passed, though, they're fighting about how to deal with her.

"Don't let her pathologize this," Jesse hears Fran hiss to Arthur on the other side of the wall. "Whatever's going on, it is not a physical illness!"

Arthur says something so rumbly and quiet that Jesse can't make it out.

"Don't be ridiculous!" Fran responds. "Once was cute, twice is a chronic behavior problem."

On the table by the Tylenol, Jesse's phone buzzes, and she reaches over her head to pick it up and see who's calling. It's Esther, for the third time already today—she must be trying Jesse between every class. Jesse's voice-mail box is crowded with unheard messages from Esther, all left since Friday evening. Zero messages from Emily, obviously. Zero messages from Wyatt, whom Jesse hasn't spoken to since he walked away from her and Esther last Wednesday—the longest they've gone without talking in years. Eleven messages from Esther, who apparently can't take a hint.

"I'm going in there," Jesse hears Fran say. Jesse quickly dismisses the call, drops the phone back onto the table, and falls back listlessly against the couch cushions.

"Kid," Fran says, rounding the doorjamb, "we have to talk."

"How are you feeling?" Arthur asks, following his wife into the room.

They stand there facing Jesse, side by side. On his forest-green sweater vest, Arthur has pinned his button from the Integrated Person Institute that reads "IT'S EASIER TO BUILD STRONG CHILDREN THAN TO REPAIR BROKEN MEN."—FREDERICK DOUGLASS. He considers Jesse with concern, stroking his beard. Fran stands with her feet spread shoulder-width apart and her arms folded tightly over her chest: lawyer-warrior stance. She's wearing the faded red baseball cap that became part of her daily uniform during her treatment, the one embroidered with the slogan NO SNIVELING.

Jesse closes her eyes. "I feel horrible."

"No doubt you do," Fran says. "It feels horrible when you flush your whole life down the toilet."

"Provoking," Arthur admonishes her quietly.

Fran ignores him. "You're upset about something, fine, that's understandable, but just because you have a reason for doing something doesn't make it justified. Everyone who commits a crime has a motive. The point is, what are the consequences of your actions?"

"Escalating," Arthur intones.

"Shrinkydink!" Fran practically shouts at her husband. "How many calls, Arthur? How many humiliating phone calls from Janet *Snediker*, of all people, do I have to field before we get a handle on this? The day that woman resigned from the No Nukes Task Force was the best day of my entire *life*, and now I have to be on the phone with her on a weekly basis, defending my daughter against the charge of deviant behavior?" She turns back to Jesse. "What do you have to say for yourself?"

"Please stop interrogating me," Jesse moans.

"Oh, this is interrogating you? Asking you legitimate questions while you lie back comfortably on your fainting couch, this is *interrogating* you?"

"Everybody's interrogating me all the time! Snediker interrogated me and now you're interrogating me—I can't get the Man off my back no matter where I go!"

It's a phrase Jesse has heard Fran use before, in a different time, in a different context. From across the room, she feels it trigger something volcanic inside her mother.

"Oh no. Oh *no*, no, no." Arthur reaches for Fran's arm, but she steps away from him and starts to pace now, working up a head of closing-argument steam. "Excuse me, no. I am not the Man. I did not march on Washington and get teargassed at Yankee Rowe nuclear plant and get screamed at doing clinic defense and get dysentery organizing sugar-cane workers in Nicaragua and spend ten years of my life working for peanuts as a public defender so I could stand in my own living room and have some fourteen-year-old kid call me the Man!"

"I'm fifteen, Mother," Jesse interjects.

"Sorry, honey, some *fifteen*-year-old kid call me the

Man. You don't know the Man, okay? You've never met the Man. The Man doesn't even live in this town! You have no idea how easy you have it, my fifteen-year-old friend, and before you get yourself thrown into juvie—which is by the way *owned* by the Man—I'm gonna need to start hearing some convincing explanations about what's behind this little misbehavior campaign of yours."

"I said I don't want to talk about it!" Jesse grabs the round, crocheted throw pillow from under her head and clamps it down over her face.

"Well, too bad. You had your twenty-four-hour reprieve. You convinced your father to let you stay home from school. Now you're gonna talk."

"Leave me alone!" Jesse shouts, muffled. "I'm sick!"

At this Fran chortles. "You are not *sick*. Believe me, I know sick, and this is not sick."

"I might not have *cancer*," Jesse snaps from under the pillow, "but I'm still *sick*."

A fine, high-pitched silence takes over the room. Jesse hears her mother exhale dangerously. Then she hears her father say, low and soothing, "Hey. Take some space. Go to the gym or something. Let me handle this."

When Jesse drags the pillow down her face a couple inches to peer over its edge, her mother is gone, and her father is sitting in the armchair opposite the couch, his elbows propped on his knees, looking at her.

"Is she mad?" Jesse asks.

Arthur smiles a little. "I believe she is."

"I shouldn't have said the cancer thing."

Arthur nods, but he doesn't absolve her. He just waits.

They sit there together, not talking, for a while. Across the room on the silent TV, a man's hand buffs a car door with a poufy white cloth. After a minute, Jesse's racing heart subsides.

"You know . . . ?" she begins tentatively. Her father nods, listening. "You know how sometimes . . . you really wish that someone would just . . . be themselves? And then they *are* themselves, and it's, like, so disappointing?"

Arthur nods thoughtfully. "Say more."

"I don't know." Jesse feels tears sting the corners of her eyes and fights to suck them back in. She doesn't make eye contact with her father, looks down at her lap. "I've been doing, like, this really bad thing. I hated doing it, but I kept doing it because I also loved it. I still sort of love it, and I still sort of wish I could keep doing it, but I can't. And also I hate that I did it. I don't know."

"You have conflicted feelings about something," Arthur offers.

Jesse nods. "I guess."

Arthur leans forward a little in his chair. "It's not drug use, is it, honey? I need you to tell me if this is drug use you're talking about."

At this Jesse cracks up a little, ruefully. "No," she says. "No." But then she thinks about it a second, about how Emily took her over physically whenever they were together, filled her with desperate craving when they were apart, made her forget her principles and sell out her friends. And gave her the most intense high she's ever experienced. In some ways, yeah, Emily Miller is a drug. And Jesse just went off her, cold turkey. No wonder she feels so hung over. "Don't worry, Dad, okay? I would totally tell you if I was doing drugs."

"I hope so." Arthur's expression is shaded with worry.

"I would. I swear to God I'm not doing drugs."

"All right. I believe you."

"It doesn't matter what it is. Forget it. It's nothing."

"I have my own theory about what's been going on with you," Arthur says. "If you don't mind my sharing it."

Jesse shrugs: *okay.*

"We talked about your mother's illness a lot while it was happening. But we haven't talked about it so much since she started to get better. One thing I'm wondering is if you're still thinking about it now. I wonder if you're realizing, now that she's healing, just how close we came to losing her."

Jesse stays very still, keeps her voice perfectly calm, when she says, "No. I'm not thinking about that."

"Okay." Arthur nods, and waits. He never expects Jesse to finish what she's saying in only one sentence.

"She's too tough to die," Jesse observes.

Arthur smiles. "That's funny, and she is very tough,

but we both know that's not really true. That's the kind of thing we say to comfort ourselves when we're feeling worried."

"I'm not feeling worried," Jesse insists, sharper this time.

"Okay. Well, I'll speak for myself, then. I've noticed that lately I feel a lot of confusing things about Mom. Sometimes right in the middle of doing something unrelated to her, right in the middle of feeling perfectly fine, I'll suddenly feel very angry or sad. Just out of nowhere, I get a big burst of sadness or anger. And I think to myself, Ah, this must be a little bit of those feelings that I had to put to the side when we were so focused on her treatment, coming back to haunt me now. You know what I'm talking about?"

"Not really. No." Jesse keeps her voice light and disengaged. "I told you, I'm not thinking about that at all. I have, like, real problems to deal with."

Arthur raises his eyebrows. "I see. Well, that's fine. We don't have to talk about this right now."

He gets up and goes to leave the room. When he's almost at the door, Jesse calls after him. "I just don't want to live in a cave, okay?"

Arthur stops and turns to look at her.

"What do you mean, 'live in a cave'?"

"I mean, I don't want to live in the dark with, like, piles of junk and garbage everywhere. No matter what happens

I just want you to always get dressed in the mornings. And sleep in your own bed."

Arthur considers his response, as always. "I don't know exactly what you're referring to," he says carefully, "but I hear that you're worried that something might happen that would cause me to neglect our daily routines. And you don't want that."

"No I don't!"

"You want me to keep taking care of myself, and you, even if something happens to disrupt our life."

"Yes."

Arthur crosses the living room to sit down on the couch beside his daughter. Jesse pulls her legs up close to her chest to make room for him, and he puts his arm around her bent knees.

"You know, I've had the funniest feeling lately, like I want to try to build something with my hands. You know how terrible I am with power tools, so nothing big, just something small for the yard. Like a birdhouse, maybe. I don't see clients until four forty-five. You want to come with me to the hardware store and get some supplies? And then maybe we can work together on a little building project?"

"Okay." Jesse leans down and puts her cheek on her father's arm. She feels him bend to kiss the back of her head.

"Something tangible," he says, into her too-long hair. "Something solid, that won't go away."

✳ ✳ ✳

Arthur holds the door to Murray and Sons Hardware open for Jesse, and it tinkles nostalgically as it falls closed behind them. The store is dark and smells like paint, tar, and chalk.

"Somewhere in here I know they've got birdhouse kits," Arthur says thoughtfully, more to himself than to Jesse. He disappears down the Plumbing and Electrics aisle, and Jesse wanders down Screws and Brackets, letting her fingertips dip into and get nipped by each box of sharp metal barbs.

"Help you, dude?" Jesse turns and looks up into the baseball-cap-shaded face of Mike McDade. When he sees her he takes a step back and begins to stammer. "Oh, sorry, I mean, sorry, I just—"

"It's cool," Jesse says automatically.

"I just, I thought you were a guy from behind." Mike is obviously flustered; he's also obviously never heard of quitting while he's ahead.

"Yeah," Jesse says. "I get it. It's cool."

Mike nods. They stand there, waiting to see what will happen next. Jesse's mind is racing. She thinks, *I've kissed her a hundred times. You've never even heard of me. Her tongue was in my mouth only days ago. You don't know anything about me. You get to kiss her today and tomorrow and probably for the rest of your*

THE DIFFERENCE BETWEEN YOU AND ME

life. I'll never touch her again. You don't even know my name.

"Jesse, right?" Mike says experimentally, pointing a little finger gun at Jesse's chest.

Surprised, Jesse nods.

"From Vander."

She nods again.

"Are you, like, one of the ones doing the whole anti-StarMart thing?" Jesse's mouth falls open in surprise. "I don't know, maybe that's not you, I don't know."

Mike swallows hard. He's more awkward than Jesse would have imagined, only having ever watched him operate from a distance. He always looked so relaxed and confident from afar. But he has a certain nerdiness to him, a certain hesitancy. It throws her off.

"Yeah," she says, "I am. I mean, I was."

"Oh, you quit?"

"I didn't—I sort of—no. No. I'm still doing it." Jesse makes a mental note to call Esther tonight and pick up where they left off.

"So it was you who put those flyers up?" Jesse nods. "Cool. Cool. I was just wondering, like, is there some way I could get involved in that?"

Jesse pauses, squints up at Mike. "You want to help fight StarMart?"

"Yeah, it's just . . ." Mike moves in a few inches toward

Jesse and lowers his voice confidentially. "You know, this place has been here, like, sixty years."

"*This* place? Murray's?"

"Yeah, like, Mr. Murray's dad started it in like the thirties. And I've been working here since eighth grade, both my brothers worked here, and Mr. Murray's such an awesome guy, he gave both my brothers money at their graduations, like, for college, and it turns out he's, like, totally against StarMart coming in. He told us this story about his friend over in Windsor who had, like, a family-owned hardware store just like this and a StarMart moved in, like, twenty miles away, not even next door or anything, but still he went under in less than six months. It happened last year. Mr. Murray was all like, 'Sixty years to build a business and six months to kill it dead.'"

Mike kneads the bill of his baseball cap with his left hand, pops the cap up off his close-cut curls, then sets it back down again. In the moment when his hair is revealed, Jesse feels a bright comet of envy streak through her chest; Mike's haircut is so perfect, so clipped and polished and clean. He has such an effortlessly cool boy-head. Jesse feels a throb of shame about her own shaggy bangs, then focuses again.

"Yeah," she says. "That's what StarMart does."

"Yeah so, Mr. Murray's been more and more worried about it lately and we've all been saying to him, like, 'Oh, Mr. Murray, your customers are loyal, they won't leave you no matter what.' But I don't know, you know? I looked at that website it said about on your flyer and I just, it seems like if StarMart comes in there's not much you can do, you know? If you're a small business like this one. And I would feel so bad if that happened here, to Mr. Murray. I just . . . I don't . . . we can't . . ."

Mike trails off, either shy or embarrassed or overwhelmed, Jesse can't tell.

"We can't let that happen to him?" Jesse supplies, and Mike's head bobs up and down vigorously.

"Right. Right. So, like, what's your plan? For defeating StarMart?"

"Oh. Um, I guess it's not really possible to actually defeat StarMart? Since they're like one of the largest corporations in the world?"

"Oh." Mike looks crestfallen. "Well, but what about just this one StarMart, just this one that might come in near us? Can we defeat that?"

When Jesse looks at Mike, she takes in the whole of him, the whole guy who has his whole body around Emily Miller whenever he wants to. For a second, the familiar feeling of being about to let something out—about to blow her cover—comes over Jesse. It's almost like having a well-known flavor of gum in her mouth. She holds the secret on her tongue, feeling its weight, tasting its comforting bittersweetness, for long enough that Mike McDade shifts uneasily.

"No?" he says. "You think it's, like, not possible?"

The simplest, most effective thing would be to say, *Look, talk to your girlfriend. She's working for them, don't you know that? Find out from her what's going on. Tell her to stop sleeping with the enemy.*

Then Jesse thinks, *Who's the enemy?*

Jesse swallows all the unsaid things. Takes a breath.

"I guess the thing we're working on," she says, "was, like, trying to convince student council that we need to divest from StarMart. Like, we shouldn't take their money and use it for school functions." Mike has assumed a doglike listening posture, leaning in with his ear turned slightly in Jesse's direction to catch her words. He nods eagerly. "So, like, if you know anyone on student council you could start there. Tell them you don't want StarMart in our school. That's one thing you can do. If you know someone."

Mike swallows uncomfortably. "I do, actually," he says, "but it's kind of like, really complicated? I can't actually be public about this? Like, I really want to help, but I can't help in school. I can't be *seen* helping."

"I get it," Jesse says. In her mind she thinks, *Great. Now even her boyfriend is telling me he can't be seen with me in public.*

"No, it's really complicated," Mike continues, "I can't really explain it because it's, like, too complicated to even explain."

"I *get* it," Jesse repeats. "You have a conflict of interest."

"What?" Mike's face clouds over with incomprehension. Then resolves. "Yes. *Yes.* I have a conflict of interest. It's a really complicated conflict of interest. But is there still, like, a way for me to pitch in . . . in, like, secret?"

"Maybe."

"Like maybe I could make some more flyers for you?"

"I don't think we need any more flyers."

Mike looks crestfallen. Then brightens again: "Or like, free tape? I could probably get you free tape or something from here. Mr. Murray would probably be into helping."

Jesse smiles. "We could maybe use free tape."

"Or other supplies, tacks, glue—whatever you wanted. Just keep me posted. Let me know what I can do." Mike bobs his head up and down, then says searchingly, "I'm not, like, generally this guy. I'm the guy who's like, 'It's none of my business to tell anyone else how to live their life.' I never even do the Juvenile Diabetes Walk, even though my brother has it and my whole family does it every year. But this, I don't know. It just feels, like, personal. I just think this is really important."

"Yeah, it is," Jesse agrees.

"So, seriously, come find me here if there's, like, anything I can do. I work Tuesday and Thursday afternoons and weekends. Or, oh!" Mike's eyes light up with a new thought. "I bet I could get the guys from baseball to participate in something. Maybe I could, I don't know. If we had snacks for them or whatever."

"That would be awesome."

"Do you do athletics?" Mike asks, friendly. He shoves his hands into his pockets and shrugs them deep down into the legs of his khakis. "You're not on softball, are you?"

Jesse smiles faintly. "Um, no."

"You should go out for it. I bet you'd be great."

"Thanks, but I suck at sports."

"You?" Mike grins. "Naw. No way."

"It's true. Some lesbians actually suck at sports."

Mike's face goes up like a boiled lobster. He blushes so deeply he's practically purple.

"I didn't, I didn't, uh—" he gropes helplessly.

At this moment, Arthur comes around the corner of the aisle.

"There you are," he says to Jesse, and Jesse says to Mike, "My dad."

"How are you, sir?" Aggressively, Mike reaches out and takes Arthur's hand, shakes it too hard and too long. Arthur looks confusedly at Jesse.

"We wanted to build a birdhouse," Arthur explains, and Mike stammers, "Birdhouse, yeah, yeah, we have kits for that!" before dropping Arthur's hand and practically bounding off toward the back of the store.

"Nice fellow," Arthur says. "Who is he?"

"My former nemesis," Jesse says, and smiles.

An hour later, Jesse and Arthur are hunched over their half-constructed birdhouse in the dusty garage, trying to figure out how to slot Roof Part A into Wall Part B.

"There must be a part missing," Arthur says tensely. His normally oceanic patience is starting to run out.

"I don't think so." Jesse consults the hieroglyphic line-drawing instructions. "See how this little pokey thing is supposed to go into that little gappy place?"

"I see that there in the instructions, yes, but I do not see it here in life." Arthur points accusingly at the half-built box.

From across the room comes the sound of Fran clearing her throat. Jesse looks up to see her mother silhouetted in the doorway, haloed by afternoon sunlight, arms crossed in her typical fashion. "Cured, I see," Fran observes.

"Oh. Hi. Yeah. I feel a lot better."

"Yes," Arthur says, flinging Roof Part A down onto the worktable a little harder than necessary. "A trip to the hardware store and a constructive hands-on project turned out to be just what the doctor ordered." He wipes the sweat off his forehead with the back of his hand. "I don't know why I'm sweating. The damn thing is only twelve inches high."

"What are you guys making?" Fran strolls into the room and approaches the worktable.

"A birdhouse, allegedly," Arthur says, the closest thing

to gruff that he ever gets. "Though at this point it's more of a bird pen."

"We can't get the roof to stick on," Jesse explains.

"Interesting problem. Arthur, could I have a moment alone with my daughter?"

Arthur brushes off his hands and steps away from the worktable. "Of course," he says. "Perfect timing. I need to wash up and get ready for clients anyway."

"Ha-ha, don't leave me alone with her," Jesse half jokes.

"Ha-ha," Arthur echoes, already on his way out.

"Yes," Fran says archly. "Ha."

After her father leaves the garage, Jesse stares deeply into the roofless birdhouse and sands its edge in vague swipes, afraid to meet her mother's eye.

"So okay," Fran begins, taking the floor. "First of all, I'm not going to ask for an apology from you about the cancer remark, even though I do think you should apologize to me for the very rude cancer remark you made earlier today."

"Are you asking me for an apology or aren't you?" Jesse looks up squarely at her mother, a challenge.

Fran breathes in and out through her nose, the calming-breath technique she learned in her stress reduction class last year. "I'm not. Even though I want to. Because I feel like there must be extenuating circumstances that led you to make that highly uncalled-for, snide remark."

Jesse shrugs. "I guess."

Fran does the calming breath again, a little less calmly this time. "Okay. So let's move on from that. I want to talk to you about a bigger issue." Fran clears her throat, then clears it again, awkwardly. "Daddy would probably want me to start by naming my feelings and using I-statements."

Jesse nods.

"So, um." Fran looks up at the raftered ceiling and blows out a sigh, as if clearing her chest of self-consciousness. "I feel that you're not learning from your mistakes."

"'Feel that' is not a true I-statement," Jesse corrects her. "True I-statements don't have 'that' in them." It's one of Arthur's cardinal rules: *feel that* doesn't really name an emotion, it introduces a judgment.

"Right, right. Okay. I feel, uh, I feel frustrated when you don't learn from your mistakes."

"That's also not a true—"

"Let me finish, okay? Will you please lay off the grammar police and let me finish? I'm trying to work up to something here. Jeez." Fran runs both hands through her short white hair. "Okay. I feel worried that you're heading down a dangerous path. I feel afraid that you're going to make a dumb mistake that will compromise your future. I feel concerned that there's something sort of major going on with you that you're not telling us about for some reason. And I feel annoyed that after all our years of hard work trying to create a safe, supportive environment for you to grow up in, you still feel like you have to keep secrets from us. Why won't you talk to us about what's really going on?"

"Why do you assume there's something 'really going on'? I got busted a couple of times by Snediker, so what? Sometimes when you do actions, there are consequences. 'If you don't end up in jail, it's not much of a principled statement,' right? Wasn't that you?"

"Sweetheart, I'm not talking about jail, I'm not even talking about the busts, I mean, I *am* talking about the busts, but it's more than that, it's . . ."

Fran trails off. She drags a paint-spattered stool over from by the wall and plunks down on it, right next to where Jesse's standing.

"Look. You're a forthright kid. You've always been an unusually direct, forthright kid. It's one of the things I admire most about you. But for a while now I've felt like you're, I don't know, jumpy. Furtive. Defensive. Weird around the house. Myron says it's just adolescence—"

"You talked to *Myron* about me?" Jesse groans. Myron is her mother's boss at the firm, the kind of chummy older dude in a rumpled sport coat who's always asking you questions about your "after-school hobbies" and socking you unpleasantly in the arm.

"Myron has three grown kids; he's a font of great advice. I talk to Myron about you all the time."

Jesse rolls her eyes. "Great."

"Myron thinks you're individuating and Daddy thinks you're pissed at me because of the cancer but I think it's something else. I think you're messed up in the head about something and I want you to talk to me about it. Talk to me about it!"

Jesse sighs her giantest leave-me-alone sigh.

Fran softens. "Please?"

Jesse turns to look at her mother. "I don't . . ." she begins, and falters. "I can't . . ."

Sitting beside her on the rickety stool, Fran's head only comes up to Jesse's chest. As she looks up at Jesse with her stormy, pleading eyes, her pure-white hair as short and glossy as a pelt, Jesse gets a vision of her as a small cartoon mouse, begging for a piece of cheese.

Jesse wants to tell her. She wants to be the direct, forthright kid that her mother wants to have raised. But every part of the story about Emily is paralyzingly embarrassing: the lying and sneaking, the mind-mangling lust, and most of all, Emily herself. Perfect, pretty, ponytailed Emily, the closeted StarMart storm trooper. If Esther is Fran's idea of Jesse's perfect girl, what would she think about Emily?

"Is it a girl?" Fran puts her hand on Jesse's knee. Jesse looks away. To her dismay, she feels her eyes fill with tears.

"It's Esther, isn't it? Sweetheart, you can tell me."

"It's not *Esther*!" Jesse gets to her feet, shaking off

Fran's hand, and strides to the other side of the table. "God! You're so presumptuous! You always think you know everything about me, but you don't know everything about me, all right?"

"All right! I concede! I hardly know anything about you! I shouldn't have assumed this was about Esther."

"It doesn't even matter who it is, because it's over." Jesse turns her attention fiercely to Roof Part A, pivoting it around and around and trying to cram it onto the bottom half of the birdhouse.

"Oh?" Fran says tentatively. Jesse can feel her adjusting her position on the little stool across the table, sitting up to pay closer attention. "But there was someone."

Jesse nods. All at once, she can feel herself getting closer to telling. It feels electric, stepping into this zone of almost-saying-it, after keeping it carefully tucked away and insulated for so long. Her mouth feels crackly with sparks, like she's holding a whole packet of Pop Rocks on her tongue.

"Someone you wouldn't approve of," Jesse says.

"How do you know I wouldn't approve of her?"

"Because she's not the kind of person you like."

Fran shakes her head, bemused. "And what 'kind' of person do I like?"

"Um, radical people?" Jesse snaps, annoyed at having to explain the obvious. "People who try to make the world

a better place? Gandhi? Thurgood Marshall? Martin Lu-
ther King Jr.? Oprah?"

"I do love Oprah." Fran smiles. "I can't help myself.
She's fabulous."

"Well, this girl isn't like that." Jesse drops Roof Part A
and starts messing with the tiny, dried-up tube of wood
glue that came in the birdhouse kit, trying to unscrew its
miniature cap.

"This girl's not like Oprah. Or Gandhi, or Thurgood
Marshall."

Jesse shakes her head. "No."

"So what *is* she like?"

"She's . . ."

How can Jesse explain Emily to her mother? How
can she describe Emily's fluid beauty, her long-legged
walk, the way her jeans fit on her hips, her laugh—
recognizable to Jesse in any crowded hallway—her hood-
ies, her V-necks, the taste of her skin, the smell of her hair,
the way she looks like she was just born to move down a
hallway in a group of girls whenever Jesse sees her from
a distance in school? How can Jesse describe this regular
girl who is somehow, in some way, haloed in magic, for no
other reason than because she's Emily Miller? "She's normal," Jesse says finally.

"And I don't like normal people?"

"It's not that, it's just—she's like, *super*normal. She's

against everything I stand for. She has a boyfriend."

"Ah." Fran nods. "I see."

"She won't admit in public that she likes me. And she works for StarMart's parent company," Jesse finishes darkly.

Fran cocks her head and squints. "Wait, how old is this girl?" she asks.

"She's a junior," Jesse says.

"A junior in high school? With a corporate job?"

"She has some kind of internship with them in Stonington, I don't know. I couldn't even listen to her when she was telling me about it, it made me so upset."

"Wow, okay. Okay." Fran gets up from her stool and paces a moment, full of energy, then turns to face Jesse. "So my first priority, obviously, is your well-being, and this relationship doesn't sound like it's been great for your well-being." Jesse shrugs. "Anyone who won't admit publicly that they're dating my daughter is obviously not good enough for her, that's how I feel. But before I dole out any motherly advice about how to handle this, let me just say: I have to hand it to you, kid. This one's a doozy." There is a note of genuine appreciation in Fran's voice. "Your girl is a closet case who works for StarMart? I've found myself in some compromising situations myself over the years, but this one is *rough*."

"*Now* you see why I couldn't tell you?"

"Actually, no, because—"

"No one has ever done anything as stupid as this, ever, in the history of the entire world!" Jesse wails, cutting her mother off.

Fran rolls her eyes. "Kid, please. Practically *everyone* in the history of the entire world has done something as stupid as this." Fran comes around now to Jesse's side of the table. "Look. You've heard me mention Daniel Karp every now and then, right?"

"Yeah, the guy Daddy hates."

Fran smiles ruefully. "Daddy does hate him, yes. Daniel Karp is the guy I was dating when I met Daddy."

"You met Daddy *while* you were dating Daniel Karp? So you dated them both at the same time?"

"Not ex*actly* . . ." Fran winces a little, seems to search the air above her for an explanation. "Not really. Sort of. It was complicated for a while there. Anyway, the point is, I was with Daniel for a couple of years before I even knew Daddy. We met arguing a case—on *opposite* sides. He was an assistant DA. Right after he lost and my client was acquitted, he came over to shake my hand and asked me out."

"Whoa."

"I know. It was ridiculous. And extremely hot."

"Please don't say 'hot.'" Jesse scrunches her shoulders up to her ears and edges away from her mother.

"I'm sorry if it makes you uncomfortable, I'm sorry if Daddy hates to hear me say it, but I'm not going to lie about it: Daniel Karp was hot. That guy was one of the most brilliant litigators I've ever seen in action. And he had incredible cheekbones. Also, he was pure evil, but that's another story."

"So fine, you're saying that everyone makes mistakes blah blah blah and I don't have to feel bad about it and I should just forget I ever met her."

"No, and please don't put words into my mouth. I wasn't going to say you should forget about her, whoever she is. Of course I don't want you to be in a situation where you have to hide, that's never going to be okay with me. For that reason alone, I'm glad it's over. But just being with someone who's wrong for you isn't necessarily a mistake. I'm certainly not sorry I was with Daniel, even though we didn't last and he drove me up a wall every freaking second we were together, because I learned a tremendous amount from being with him. And we were totally into each other, right up until the end, even though we could never really figure out why."

Jesse sighs. "I just . . . I just hate feeling so dumb. I *know* better than to like her. I *don't* like her. And I don't even *get* to like her anymore. But I just . . ." Jesse looks down at the floor. "I just *like* her. It makes me feel like a tool."

"Once," Fran says, settling against the worktable and folding her arms, "I knew this kid who very bravely and bossily came out of the closet when she was only fourteen years old. She told me then that we can't choose who we love. We just love the people we love, no matter what anyone else might want for us. Wasn't that you?"

17

Emily

Obviously, I made the right decision to put a little distance between me and Jesse. I sort of took my own self by surprise when I said it—I certainly didn't go into school that morning thinking I was going to tell her we should take a break. But when I saw her there outside the dean's office, it just popped out of my mouth, and as soon as I said it I knew it was the right thing to do.

Some of the most important things that happen in a person's life are split-second decisions. Sometimes it's in those quick moments, when your brain sort of does something without your permission, where you can be the most brave.

Like—ironically—the first time I kissed Jesse. It was an accident, sort of. It happened during Vander Open House Night, which is an evening event for parents and guardians held at the beginning of every year, where your parents or guardians come to school and run through a short version of your schedule and get a chance to meet your teachers and experience a snapshot of your life as a Vander student.

Most kids don't come to Open House Night—it's not a student event—but I was there volunteering as a student council representative, and Jesse was there for some other random reason, maybe representing some LGBTQ student group that doesn't exist anymore? To be honest, I don't know why she was there, but she was. And during the fake lunch period when all the parents gather in the cafeteria to have school-made snacks while Mr. Greil gives them a talk about the importance of parental involvement, Jesse and I both ended up in the girls' room in the sophomore hall.

We were the only ones in there. We were standing side by side at the sinks. It was so weird to be in the sophomore hall girls' room at night. It's usually so bright and sunny in there, because of the high windows, but the little fluorescent strips that are over the mirrors barely do a thing to light the room when it's dark, it turns out. We could hardly even see our reflections in the dimness.

We were both looking at ourselves in the mirror, and then we were looking at each other in the mirror.

I had seen her around. I was curious about her. But I never expected her to *say* anything to me. I don't know what made her feel like she could talk to me that night. Maybe she didn't expect me to say anything back.

We were kind of looking at each other, but we hadn't

even said hi, and all of a sudden she was like, "I like your hair."

Okay. Lots of girls have said nice things to me about my hair or my outfits or whatever over the years. Thousands of girls, probably. Millions. But when Jesse said it, it didn't sound like anything that any other girl had said to me before. It had a different meaning. It made my stomach flutter. It was like Jesse had seen something inside me that no one else had ever seen, and complimenting my hair was her way of telling me she'd seen it. It was like a secret code I'd never heard before, but somehow automatically understood.

If you asked me what I said back to her then, or what she said back to me after that, or what the next couple of things were that happened that night, I couldn't tell you. All I know is that I made the first move. I led her into one of the stalls in the girls' room and that's where we kissed for the first time.

I remember it smelled like damp, rotten paper towels. I remember that my insides tumbled over and over the instant she touched me. I remember thinking, *This is incredible.* And also, *This can never happen again.*

That boldness that sometimes takes you over before your brain tells you to stop, it can change your life in incredible ways. It can make you stand up for yourself when you need to most, and take big risks, and really put yourself out there. But it can also screw everything up for you.

I'm not saying I don't miss her. I totally miss her. I sort of feel like my life has gone gray all over since I told her we should take a break. Last Tuesday at work I felt so sick to my stomach shelving in the third-floor stacks that I ended up asking Carol if I could leave an hour early. I couldn't wait to be out of that library. I couldn't stand being up on the third floor, knowing that she wasn't there, too.

But sometimes you have to weigh the pros and cons of a situation and make a really hard decision. Sometimes the kind of brave you have to be isn't split-second, change-your-life brave, it's big-picture, think-about-your-future brave. Sometimes you have to sacrifice something you love, if you don't want to lose everything you have.

18

Jesse

"We could try to get people to boycott?" Esther suggests. "All the people who signed our petition, we could send them emails telling them to, like, boycott something."

She's sitting on Jesse's unmade bed after school on Thursday, brainstorming possible actions for the night of the Starry Starry Night Dance, working through the plate of Fig Newtons that Fran insisted they take upstairs ("Strategizing fuel!" she said just now in the kitchen, as she foisted the plate on Esther). Jesse is standing across the room from Esther in front of the bureau, examining herself critically in the mirror.

Jesse expected Esther to be annoyed at having left so many unreturned messages, but when she called her to make a plan for Esther to come over and work on the anti-StarMart campaign, Esther was totally cheerful about it. They picked up right where they left off: same enthusiasm, no tension.

"But what should they boycott? Boycotts don't do much unless someone's already been paying for something, right?" Jesse thinks out loud. She runs her hands through her hair experimentally, making it stick up from her forehead and fall back down in different shapes.

"What about . . . what about . . ." Esther chews on a Newton. "What about a picket line?"

"I feel like that's uncool," Jesse says vaguely.

"Yeah, I guess, me too. I was just trying to think of what we could do that would distract people from the dance and teach them the truth about StarMart at the same time. Hey, how about a teach-in? Phyllis from the vigil runs a really fantastic teach-in."

Jesse has been to at least a dozen teach-ins in her life, group-run lecture sessions on topics ranging from natural gas exploration to the death penalty to nuclear waste storage. They tend to be pretty grim affairs: a bunch of already-angry people in a room trying to convince each other to be even angrier. Sometimes they have snacks: apple juice and generic sandwich cookies. They do not, as a rule, compete with a dance for fun and entertainment value.

"Maybe. I don't know. Teach-ins are kind of boring. We need something exciting that will make people pay attention to us on the same night they were planning to just dance and make out."

Esther looks up from the plate of Newtons, eyes wide. "I've got it. We can have our own dance!"

"I don't know. . . ."

"No, a counterdance! A dance to end StarMart! This is the perfect idea! We can have it in the parking lot! Or in Huckle's backyard! Or both! And we can have music and snacks, and people can give a dollar to get in, and we can gather all the money and donate it to someone, like to Arlo and Charlie for their new organization."

"Arlo and Charlie don't have an organization."

"Not yet, but what if we raised a bunch of money for them? And they could use it to fight StarMart? This is an awesome idea, Jesse. Admit it: a counterdance is an awesome idea."

"I hate dances," Jesse says. "They're totally gender-oppressive and awful."

"Yeah, but ours wouldn't be. Ours would be tolerant and open. We could invite everybody, not just the school. We'll send an Evite to every single name on the petition! We can even put it in the paper and invite the whole community. Oh my God, I'm so excited, this is perfect. This is perfect!"

Esther has taken a little notebook out of her book bag and is writing something across the top of one page in big letters.

"To do!" she crows.

"It sounds like a lot of hard work," Jesse says listlessly.

"Yes, I love hard work." Esther is scribbling furiously in her notebook now, bearing down with her pen so hard that the paper tears a little as she writes. "Okay, so first category on the list: supplies. One, tent. Giant tent. No idea where we can get a giant tent. We'll find out. Two, folding chairs. I have a couple, and I know where we can get some more. Three—hey, excuse me, what are you *doing*?"

Jesse is holding a fistful of shaggy blonde hair up off the top of her head with her left hand and beginning to saw away at it with the Swiss Army Knife in her right. "Haircut?" she explains.

"You can't do it like that!" Esther puts her pen and notebook down on the bed beside her and jumps to her feet, appalled.

"This is how I do it," Jesse says. "I cut my own hair all the time."

But Esther says, "Give me that." She crosses the room swiftly, takes the Swiss Army Knife from Jesse, snaps it shut, and puts it down on Jesse's cluttered desk.

"You can't cut your hair with a blunt instrument, it damages it. My mom would have passed out if she saw you doing that."

"Your mom was into hair?"

"She was a cosmetologist. When I was little she used to see ladies privately at our house, for cuts and wash-and-sets and stuff. She used to let me take out their curlers when they were done sitting under the dryer. Their curls were all dry and hot and crispy before she combed them out."

"Ew," says Jesse.

"Yeah," Esther agrees. "My mom always said that you can make someone a better person by giving them the right hairdo. She thought that a lot of people were depressed just because they didn't know how to do their hair right."

"It's sort of true, though. The second my hair gets too long I feel kind of embarrassed by it or something. I feel grossed out. That's why I started cutting it myself. I couldn't wait around for my mom to take me to Styles by Felice every time I needed a trim."

"Let me cut it for you." Esther reaches out and runs her fingers through Jesse's scruff-head, teasing it up and smoothing it down. It's a surprising gesture. Jesse almost pulls away, but stops herself.

"You?"

"Relax, I know what I'm doing. You need to wet your whole head. And find me a pair of real scissors. No jack-knifes."

When Jesse comes back from the bathroom, head dripping, towel around her neck, and scissors in her hand, Esther sits her down in the desk chair and stands behind her. She towels Jesse's head off roughly, making it flop around on her neck like a scarecrow's. Then she says, "Don't worry. This will only hurt a bit."

"Short," Jesse warns her. "Really short."

"I know, I know. Really short."

Esther moves around Jesse, tugging at her hair so hard

that her head jerks back and forth in the directions Esther pulls it in. It doesn't hurt, even though it's rough, and Esther's hands on her head are warm and strong. After a bit Jesse surrenders to the yanking and pushing. Her head gets heavy on her neck, and she starts to slip down a little in her chair.

"Tip your chin down," Esther commands. Jesse does. "The last time I was touching somebody's hair, I was shaving my mom's head for her. That was a while ago."

Jesse's face is tipped down and to one side. She stares at her own chest. "Oh."

"Did your mom shave her head when she got sick?"

"First she dyed her hair bright purple. Then she shaved her head."

"Cool. I can tell she's the kind of person who would do something like that. She's not scared of being open about things. That must have made it easier on you to have her sick."

Easier? Jesse thinks. "Maybe. She wasn't exactly easy. But she did love being bald. She really got off on being the crazy bald-headed lady with no eyelashes at, like, the Barnes and Noble. My dad was always trying to get her to wear a hat so she wouldn't get cold, but she liked being bald in public. She liked making a statement. The hat she wore at home."

"Brave," Esther murmurs.

"Yeah. Or just, like, a giant pain in the ass."

Esther giggles. "My mom went wig shopping the day after she was diagnosed. She was such a modest person but she was vain about her hair. She used to say, 'It's my best asset.' Losing her hair was the worst thing for her about cancer. In the beginning, anyway."

"Yeah."

Esther snips away at the base of Jesse's neck, tidying her hairline there. The scissors nip at Jesse's skin, and make quiet little slicing noises every time they close.

"I miss her a lot."

"I bet."

"Look up."

Jesse lifts her chin, and Esther moves around to stand in front of Jesse. She bends down and stares into Jesse's face abstractly, scanning it for shape and symmetry, not looking into her eyes.

"It's weird the times I miss her most. You'd think it would be at night right before I fall asleep or something, but it's all different, strange other times, like when I'm waiting for a bus. I remember her a lot when I'm waiting for a bus, I think because it reminds me of when I used to wait for her to pick me up. Or like, right now, even. She would love the counterdance idea. She was really into planning parties. She was head of the events committee at church and she always knew where to buy the best cheap decorations and how to work all the different coffee urns. Hey,

coffee urn, we have to put that on the list." Esther drops
the scissors, wipes her wet hands on Jesse's neck towel,
and goes for her pen and notebook on the bed. She shoves
them into Jesse's hand and resumes cutting her hair without missing a beat.

"Do people usually have a coffee urn at a dance,
though?" Jesse wonders.

"Maybe people don't, usually, but we should," Esther
says confidently. "It'll be cold out, and people will want coffee. We want them to stay, right? And have a great time?
And learn about how StarMart wants to destroy our town?"

"Yeah."

"So we have to give them coffee and snacks. My mom
always got Vienna Fingers."

Esther folds down Jesse's right ear and snips around it
delicately.

"We could get those." Jesse drops her head farther to
the side to give Esther more ear access.

"And we need excellent music. Who do you know who
likes music and could play music for us? What about your
friend Wallace?"

"Who?"

"With the cowboy pants?"

"Wyatt. We're sort of not talking right now."

"Oh no, why not?"

"I don't actually know."

"Well, listen," Esther says briskly, "if we want to put together a whole dance in just a couple of weeks? We're going to need all the help we can get. You should call him and make up with him. Get him to help."

"He hates music," Jesse says, "but I'll try."

Esther takes a sharp snip at Jesse's bangs and steps back.

Together, Jesse and Esther turn to look at Esther's handiwork in the mirror.

"Awesome," says Jesse. "Perfect."

All at once, there she is again: Jesse as she should be, Jesse as she knows herself best, sleek and shorn, right and ready.

19

Jesse

When Jesse opens the door to Beverly Coffee on the morning of Saturday the thirtieth, she spots Wyatt sitting at a little table against the wall, reading *Atlas Shrugged* determinedly. It's dim and quiet in the café, and pretty empty for a Saturday. At one table an old man in a fedora reads a newspaper and takes dainty sips from a demitasse. At another table, two college kids are studying, big fat books spread out between them.

Jesse stands for a second in the doorway and takes Wyatt in from across the room, his extremely familiar mop of dark curls, the unmistakable curve of his neck and shoulders as he bends his head to read. His Western outfit has given way already to a badly beaten leather bomber jacket, cracked all over and with the lining coming loose at the collar, and some kind of nylon cargo pants with pockets up and down the side of the leg. He occupies the chair gracefully, his posture assembled and still, but Jesse knows him well enough to spot the light tremors of anxiety moving through his extremities—the thumb of his right hand riffling the corner of his book over and over again, the heel of his long, black Converse high-top bouncing up and down on the tile floor.

Wyatt is so familiar to her, like a family member. Like her own face in the mirror. The sight of him fills her with warmth, recognition, and guilt.

She crosses to the table where he is and sits down opposite him. He looks up sharply, but his eyes widen with surprise when he sees Jesse.

"Oh. Hi."

"Hi," Jesse says.

"I can't really talk right now. Howard's gonna show up any second."

"I know, that's why I'm here."

"I assumed you weren't coming."

"I said I would. I promised."

"And then you disappeared."

Jesse nods. "Yeah. I'm really sorry," she offers. "I know I've been weird."

Wyatt nods back and waits for more. Jesse swallows, mustering her courage.

"It's just that I've been, like, distracted by something and feeling guilty about it, and wanting to tell you about it but feeling like I couldn't tell you. But I want to tell you now."

"Let me guess: you're in love."

There's an unmistakable note of sarcasm in Wyatt's voice. Jesse waits a moment before she says, "Actually, yeah. Or I was."

"Oh, it's over already? That was quick. What's her name again? Myrtle? Hortense?"

"Esther? It's not Esther, why does everyone think I'm with Esther?"

"Maybe because the two of you keep cuddling up like lovers while you walk around town?"

"I don't—I never *cuddled up* to her, and she's not—I only like Esther as a friend!"

"Too bad, you guys are clearly the perfect couple. You can spend the rest of your lives bringing student councils to their knees together."

Jesse breathes.

"Can you maybe not be mean to me right now, while I'm trying to, like, tell you something that's really hard for me to talk about?"

"I'm sorry, I guess I'm not in the perfect mood to hear a big confession from you while I'm sitting here waiting for Howard. You've been ignoring me for, like, weeks, and this is not the first time you've done this to me. You keep disappearing into wormholes where I can't find you. It's like you're here one second and gone the next. Frankly, it's getting tiresome."

"Well, honestly? To be honest? I sort of feel like you've been doing that, too."

"I'm right here," Wyatt says curtly.

"I know, but like . . . the Denmark thing?"

"I don't even know if I'm going to do that, it's just an idea!"

"And you're not in school anymore."

"You *know* why that is."

"I know and I'm sorry, but you're sort of completely gone. So many parts of my life you don't know about anymore."

"Because you're keeping them from me!" Wyatt raises his voice now, his cheeks flushed. The students at the table across the room lift their heads to look at them, and Wyatt hunches over, quiets down again. "It's been totally obvious that you've been hiding some huge secret from me for months, and I let you not talk about it because I know what that can be like. But if you're not even going to call me back? Seriously, I'm over it."

"You knew?"

"Give me a little credit, will you? This is *me*." Wyatt points to his chest. "So who is it? Is it Carol Bernstein?" he asks.

"Carol Bernstein, the *reference* librarian? Wy, she's, like, sixty!"

"I know, but you're always at your weirdest in the library. I thought maybe Carol Bernstein had cast some magical reference spell over you and made you into her secret boy-toy."

"Gross. Seriously, gross. It's Emily Miller."

Wyatt gives her a blank look, then shakes his head. "Don't know her."

"No, you don't. She's a junior. She's student council vice president."

"Did you bring her to her knees in the meeting?"

"Shut up," Jesse says, mortified.

But Wyatt laughs at his own joke. "God, that's it? That's the big secret? I thought it was going to be, like, a married woman or something."

"She has a boyfriend," Jesse says.

"Oh."

"And she made me swear not to tell anyone we were hooking up."

"That's no fun."

"God, Wy, I felt so awful being with her. I mean, I felt, like, amazing? But I felt like such a bad queer."

"Well, you are a bad queer."

"I know, right?"

"But you're not the first queer to go bad like that. By any means. You remember Rob Strong?"

"Yeah?" Wyatt's tormenter is still in school with Jesse—she sees him in the halls all the time, surrounded

by a herd of his buddies or shooting the breeze in the
cafeteria with Mr. Angel, the auto-shop teacher.

"Not my finest moment." Wyatt examines the back of
his hand intently.

"Wait, *what*? No, ex*cuse* me, what?" Jesse is stunned.
The whole history of the past two years is reorienting itself in front of her eyes.

"It was just a couple times, nothing serious, but he
made me promise that I—" At this moment, the door to
the café opens, and Howard Willette walks in. Wyatt's airy
look evaporates off his face. He tightens and straightens.
"Howard's here."

"To be continued?" Jesse hisses.

Wyatt nods, but he's looking up at his father.

"Hi, Howard."

Howard Willette is a shorter, stockier, straighter version of Wyatt. They have the same dark handsomeness,
the same angular features, and the same attentive dress—
Howard is clean-cut casual, but very carefully attired in a
black jacket, lavender Oxford shirt, and black sweater vest
atop his black corduroys. He crosses to them and extends
his hand to his son.

"Wyatt."

They shake, and Wyatt tucks his book into his bag on
the floor by his feet.

"And Jesse. Always nice to see you."

"Hi," Jesse says. Immediately, she slips into Howard

Mode, plastering a cheerful smile across her face and nodding pleasantly.

"Tea? Hot cocoa?"

"I'm good," says Wyatt.

"None for me, thank you," coos Jesse.

Howard pulls a third rickety chair over to sit between them, and as soon as he's seated, Jesse fires up the conversation, as per the plan.

"So how's everything over at your place, Mr. Willette? How's Louise?"

"Great, great." Howard nods. "We're both great. And you, Jesse? What have you been up to lately?"

Wyatt looks at Jesse with mock sincerity. "Yes, what *have* you been up to lately, Jesse?"

"Oh, the usual," Jesse practically sings. "Homework, homework, and more homework!"

"The life of a hardworking sophomore," Howard says. "That's how it goes at Vander. Not like where you go, right, son? The Academy of Smelling Salts and Astrology? No homework there."

"We don't have to talk about school," Jesse offers.

But Wyatt says acidly, "I'm working my way through the complete published papers of Alan Greenspan right now. I'm learning about supply-side economics and deregulation and how they affect entrepreneurship in the tech sector."

"Wyatt's the most hardworking student I know," Jesse

hurries to point out. "He's very self-directed, and he's al-ways giving himself huge, hard assignments, way huger and harder than anything they give us at Vander. He's kicking ass."

For a second she's afraid the word will offend Howard, but he sails right by it.

"Well, you may be right. It does seem like that school is going soft. We've gotten mired in a little battle for hearts and minds over there recently, but it's—wait, never mind. Boring PR story." Howard holds up his hand to check him-self with a charming, self-deprecating smile.

"What do you mean, battle for hearts and minds?" Jesse asks.

"Never mind. Wyatt hates stories about work."

"But a story about Vander?" Jesse asks Wyatt, hyper-politely. Wyatt gives her a look: *Whatever keeps the con-versation running.*

"Well, it's nothing, really," Howard explains casually. "Nothing we haven't seen before. We reached out to them with some support for their athletics programs and extra-curricular activities and we're getting some minor push-back from the community, a couple of letters from parents, a few disgruntled hippie students who've gotten bored with throwing red paint on ladies in fur coats and have decided to move on to us as their new randomly chosen target. The school is happy to have us, though, that's the main thing. We've got plenty of support in the administration. It's going to be a long, fruitful partnership for us over there, I'm sure."

On her side of the table, Jesse is turning this story over like a multisided die in her mind. "So, um, are you talking about StarMart?" she asks as calmly as she can manage.

"Well, NorthStar, we're the parent company of StarMart, yes. I'm the director of corporate communications over there. But I can see my son's eyes glazing over here, am I right, Wyatt? You know what's a great story is the latest update on the rabbit wars. Jesse, you know that Louise has been in the middle of a battle for the sanctity of our garden, and she's come up with the cleverest way to—"

"I'm one of the disgruntled hippies," Jesse blurts out.

Across the table, Wyatt's face constricts with dread.

"Oh, you are?" Howard turns an extra-dazzling smile on Jesse. "You signed that little petition?"

"I wrote it," Jesse says.

Now Wyatt drops his head, weary.

"Interesting." Howard maintains his comfortable smile. "Very interesting. So you don't believe that your school should benefit from our generosity."

"I think StarMart has ulterior motives."

"We don't have to talk about work," Wyatt says hopefully, but Howard plows on.

"Ulterior motives, meaning that we want to become part of this community? It's true that we do want to become part of this community, and forming relationships with members of the community is one of the most important parts of that process."

"But public schools shouldn't take money from corporations," Jesse counters.

"Bunnies?" Wyatt tries to interrupt.

"Public schools have been taking contributions from private individuals and corporations for hundreds of years, it's a time-honored practice. That's not something you learn if you go to the various quote unquote research sites you refer to in the text of that petition. And you know," Howard says, settling comfortably into his seat, propping his right foot up on his corduroyed left knee, "there are a lot of people out there who don't know the truth about North-Star and who spread misinformation about us around to try to undermine us, and honestly that's why I love my job. Because every day I have the chance to go out there and let uninformed people like you, Jesse, know the real story about this company I believe in so strongly."

"Um, I'm actually not uninformed," Jesse says.

"You are, in fact, naïve and ignorant, if you're the author of that petition, but it's all right. It's not your fault."

"She's not naïve and ignorant," Wyatt says, suddenly steely.

"I don't mean it in a judgmental way, son. She's like a lot of people out there, she doesn't have the facts. Let me tell you two something about the way the world works."

"No, don't!" Wyatt snaps. "Please don't tell us about the way the world works."

Jesse watches with concern as Wyatt begins to implode internally across the table from her.

"Um," she says, "maybe this is a bad thing for us to talk about after all. I have like a great new joke for you guys, if you—"

But Howard continues with perfect patience. "Excuse me, you don't have to be rude to me, Wyatt. I'm trying to have a civil conversation with you and your friend, and I don't appreciate being shouted down when I'm trying to speak."

"I feel a lecture about values coming on," says Wyatt, "and I just want to, like, head it off at the pass before it starts."

"Okay," Jesse says, panicky. "Okay, okay—"

Howard shakes his head. "I do not lecture you about values. I have never lectured you about values."

"You lecture me about values every time I see you!"

"I respect you enough to tell you the truth about my beliefs and to make clear to you the objections I have about your problematic life choices, but I do not lecture you about—"

"Right now, right now you're starting to do it! Problematic life choices! And you called Jesse ignorant!"

"It's okay," says Jesse, but Wyatt scoops his backpack off the floor and gets to his feet.

"We don't have to do this anymore, really," he tells his father. "If we never meet like this again, it'll be fine with me. Come on, Jesse."

"Sorry," Jesse says to Howard as she follows Wyatt out the door.

"See you next month," Howard replies drily.

* * *

In the mildewy button-down-shirt aisle of Rose's Turn, Jesse follows a couple of paces behind Wyatt, fingering collars. Still coursing with rage, Wyatt flips through shirts fiercely, flicking the hangers along the pole with a metallic *click. Click. Click.*

"Horrible," he declares. "All horribly ugly. Anyway, I don't even need a shirt. I need a scarf. Where are their scarves? Where are their freaking *scarves*?"

"In the, um, scarf aisle?" Jesse says timidly.

Wyatt ignores her. *Click. Click. Click.*

"Wyatt, I'm sorry. I shouldn't have said anything." Wyatt shrugs. "My job is to tell jokes, not to start fights. I know."

"It's not your fault. He's a congenital idiot."

"Yeah. It was nice of you to stand up for me, though."

"I couldn't let him talk to you like that. He wants to call me a sinner and a pervert, fine, but I'm not going to let him insult my best friend."

THE DIFFERENCE BETWEEN **YOU** AND **ME**

Jesse bumps up against Wyatt a little, shoulder-to-shoulder. A closed-arm hug.

"Hey. Me and Esther are putting together this thing," she says, "in a couple of weeks. This, like, dance?"

"I hate dances," Wyatt responds automatically.

"I know, they're totally gender-oppressive and awful, but this one is going to be super awesome. We're holding it in the parking lot of Vander as like, an alternative to the StarMart dance. You should come."

"Do I have to physically dance?"

"You could just stand there. Actually, we still need a DJ. You want to DJ for us? In your excellent new scarf, once you find it?"

"As you're aware," Wyatt says, "I loathe popular music."

"Yeah, but you know how to work an iPod, right? I'll set up the playlists, you just need to press PLAY. It's going to be a ton of fun. And you can hang out with me and Esther. Can you handle that?"

"I can press PLAY," Wyatt says.

20

Jesse

On the morning of the dances, two weeks later, Jesse wakes up extremely early, before dawn. The sky is a cold ink-blue through the window across from the foot of her bed, and a single star hangs right where Jesse can see it from her pillow, just above the slate gable of the Claussens' roof across the street. It's a piercingly bright pinpoint of light, and it seems to throb slightly as Jesse looks at it, like a pulsar.

Jesse lies perfectly still for a couple of minutes in the deep quiet, suspended in thought and time. Her body feels long, strong, and smooth under the covers. Her mind is still. Somewhere just outside the sphere of her mind and body is the reality of what's going to happen today. It floats closer to Jesse, and closer, moving around her in a sparkly cloud of excitement.

Jesse closes her eyes for a moment, suffused with the starry anticipation of what's in store, and when she opens them again her room is washed with gray light. She must have fallen back to sleep—now the day is on. Jesse sits bolt upright in bed, her mind suddenly racing with the things she has to do. Pick up donuts and day-old cakes at Beverly Coffee. Meet Esther at Murray and Sons at nine o'clock to collect the cables and clip-lights they're borrowing. Call Wyatt to check on the sound system ETA. Extension cords, don't forget the bag of extension cords from Dad's worktable in the basement, and call Esther and remind her to bring the ones from her house, too. Tape, tape, tape—masking, Scotch, and duct. Don't forget scissors. Don't forget rope. Don't forget to load the folding table into the back of Mom's Camry so she can bring it over to Vander later. Don't forget to get the Christmas lights down from the attic.

When Jesse shows up at Murray's at ten minutes past nine, Esther is sitting cross-legged on the sidewalk to the right of the door, reading. She's in her bulky coat with a ski hat on her head, and apparently, the October chill doesn't bother her. Jesse is already a little strung out—Beverly Coffee doesn't open till ten, it turns out, so she and Esther will have to go back there after this to get the refreshments. She can't believe she's already behind on her jobs.

"Why didn't you go in already?" she asks Esther, mildly miffed.

"I was reading," Esther explains. "And waiting for you."

"It doesn't feel like we're changing the world," Jesse

says as they head into the store. "It feels like we're running a million dumb errands."

"I guess one thing feels a lot like the other." Esther grins.

For better or worse, Mike McDade isn't working this morning. But Mr. Murray himself is there, and he greets Jesse warmly when she introduces herself. Mr. Murray is a grandfatherly guy with a mustache and a cardigan, only one button of which closes over his round belly. He smells strongly of cigars, the same cigars, no doubt, that have rasped his voice into a gravelly growl.

"Here's what I got for you guys," Mr. Murray says, sliding a big cardboard box—marked HALBERSTAM in Sharpie on one side—across the countertop toward the two of them. "Mike said you just wanted the lighting stuff, right? Take a look in there and see if you want me to throw in anything else." Esther and Jesse peer into the box, which is filled to the brim with neatly coiled electric cables, metal clip-lights, and surge protector strips.

"Thanks," Jesse says. "It's perfect. Thank you so much, Mr. Murray."

"Don't thank me, I'm thanking *you*. Have a very nice party, girls. And make a lot of money for your cause."

The day is gray and clammy, and it goes by in a blur of details. Jesse and Esther hammer tent poles into Huckle's lawn, run extension cords through Huckle's windows, cram day-old donuts into their mouths, share day-old donuts with Huckle, figure out Wyatt's speaker system, and work with Arlo, who shows up at four, to lay out eight big pieces of plywood on the grass for people to dance on.

The dance floor was Arlo's idea—his collective always puts out plywood on the lawn whenever they throw a party—but still he kvetches about it the whole time they're setting it up.

"I need you to please take excellent care of this plywood," he instructs them. "This is the collective's plywood and it was difficult to salvage and we're using it again next Saturday for our straightedge rave, so please pay attention and make sure it doesn't get stolen or harmed in any way."

But after they're done working he doesn't leave. Jesse notices him mooning around the edges of the tent, thumbing his BlackBerry, picking at the nearly empty Beverly Coffee box, and waiting for the party to start.

As it gets darker and darker, Jesse gets more and more excited. At six o'clock, her mother brings by the coffee urns and hot cocoa–making supplies they're borrowing from Esther's church. At six thirty, Arthur comes with an armload of stuff: thermoses of black bean soup for Jesse and Esther; a bunch of extra hats and mittens from the hall closet; the still-roofless birdhouse, to be used as a cash box; and Jesse's light blue tuxedo, which she left by the front door in a shopping bag this morning so her father could bring it to her tonight, in time to change before the party starts. At six forty-five, dressed up now and ready to host, Jesse plugs in the last extension cord in Huckle's front hallway, and the inside of the tent—filled with clip-lights and strung with a crisscrossed web of Christmas lights—glows like a giant canvas lantern.

At seven o'clock, people start to come.

Emily

I knew about the alternative dance, of course. Everybody knew about it. People were reposting the invitation all over the place, and they even ran a notice about it in the paper. It wasn't a surprise.

I was a little bit surprised by how many people from school ended up going over there. Not hundreds of people or anything, not everyone, and not for the whole night, but a kind of surprising number of people spent at least some time out there in Jesse's tent. Which I was really glad about for her. Even after everything we'd been through, and even though we'll never, ever agree about NorthStar, I could still guess that her dance must have been really important to her. I'm the first person to support students doing all different kinds of activities to help out the causes they believe in. (As long as they respect each other and don't try to undermine each other's events or start misin-formation campaigns about each other around school, or things like that.) I guess what really surprised me was how many people didn't mind that Jesse's dance was outside. It was such a chilly night out, and I didn't expect people to want to go hang out under a tent when it was so cold. I wouldn't have thought people would enjoy dancing all night in their coats like that.

The Starry Starry Night Vander High School Fall Formal, which was held inside the gym like always, was an incredible success. It seemed like at least as many people came this year as last year, maybe one or two fewer, I didn't get the actual numbers. And anyway, the *quality* of everything at this year's dance was vastly, vastly superior to last year. It was an incredibly beautiful event, thanks to NorthStar but also, even more important, I think, thanks to the hard work that people like me and Michael and the members of the student council Fall Formal committee put in to turn our gym into a beautiful autumn wonderland.

Some of the highlights of the themed décor: realistic fake fall leaves spread rakishly on every surface, helium-filled balloons in warm fall colors arranged in bunches on either side of all the doors and in an arch over the souvenir photo-booth area, frozen punch rings floating in the faux-crystal punch bowls, and a slowly morphing projection of trees turning from green to orange to red to gold that we had going constantly on the wall behind the basketball hoop. People were unanimous about how fantastic and sophisticated everything looked.

I had originally planned to have a professional DJ, Phil

Holland, who does music for the events at the Women's Club where my mom belongs, cover the dance, but he ended up getting a high-paying job on a river cruise that night, and I had to talk Mark Salfrezi into bringing his iPod again. But he and I had a meeting beforehand about the playlists and appropriate outfits for DJing that would fit in with the evening's theme, and in the end he looked and sounded great. Practically professional.

People danced like crazy. People really, really enjoyed the donated brownie bites, and the other store-bought snacks that Michael and I had picked out. We didn't run out the whole night, and we never had to ration like last year. People really appreciated that.

At about eight o'clock, when I took over manning the snack table from Kimmie Hersh, I realized that I was standing in exactly the same spot I had been in last year when Jesse came striding through the door in her crazy tuxedo. I caught myself looking over at the door every time it opened, to see if she would come through it again, even though I knew that was ridiculous—she would never leave her own event and come over to mine. Not now. A year ago, when she came into the gym through that door, it was one of the most powerful moments in my life. Everything changed for the better that night. And even though I knew it was totally, absolutely not going to happen, I guess I thought that maybe, if she somehow came through those doors again tonight, everything would change again, and go back to how it was.

I was standing there alone at that snack table for I don't know how long, watching the doors open and close, open and close, with Jesse not coming through them. After a while, I started to feel kind of panicky, and I looked over to the souvenir photo-booth area by the wall to find Michael. One of the key things that NorthStar donated to us was a fantastic new photo printer that allowed us to take fancy pictures and print them out right there for people to take home. We had little gold card-stock sleeves with the Vander logo and NorthStar logo printed side by side on the back and the words STARRY STARRY NIGHT embossed on the other front, and the pictures slipped inside. It was such a great take-home gift. I had put Michael in charge of running the whole operation, along with a couple of other guys I knew he got along with. But when I looked over to find him right then, he was gone. There was no one in charge of souvenir pictures. No one was preserving our memories anymore.

Jesse

Jesse wanders a little ways off away from the tent, hovering in the dark where Huckle's yard meets the edge of the Vander parking lot, and looks back at the counterdance.

The Christmas lights wrapped around the tent poles and strung across the dance floor make everything look spangled and festive, but cheap and fun at the same time. The star garlands she and Esther cut out of yellow construction paper are a little wonky—some of them look more like blob garlands, and Esther went so insane with the glitter that light showers of gold sparkles sift down onto the crowd every time the garlands catch a breeze.

It's cold, but nobody seems to mind. People are jumping around happily to the music—Wyatt (in full Charles Lindbergh drag now: bomber jacket, aviator cap, goggles, scarf, lace-up boots) has some old-school No Doubt on at this moment, buoying the crowd on its bouncy ska beat. Some people don't have their coats on anymore—they've thrown them onto the folding chairs or the grass at the edge of the plywood dance floor.

It's a super mixed-up, random crowd. It certainly doesn't look like a high school dance, more like a weirdo wedding reception, with people of all ages and from all sectors of town jumping up and down together—spinning, shaking, twisting—or standing around in groups at the edge of the dance floor, chatting and drinking cocoa. All kinds of crazy people are here. Carol Bernstein, reference librarian from the Minot. Dr. Paul Klang, Jesse's dentist. Several of the other therapists who share space with her dad at his professional building—Susan, Joanne, Windsong, and Jill. Jesse's old preschool teacher Mrs. Hoyt. Bethany from Beverly Coffee. Marla from Rose's Turn. Dr. Fayed the veterinarian. Lots of people Jesse has never seen before—a group of girls who could be sorority sisters from the university in Stonington. A couple of middle-aged couples—maybe parents of Vander kids—in his-and-hers Patagonia fleece jackets. A young dad spinning around and around in a floppy, knitted hunter's cap, with a stunned-looking baby strapped to his chest wearing its own tiny replica of the cap. Lots and lots of kids from school—random kids, most Jesse recognizes but some she doesn't. Ralphie Lorris. Black-Haired-Bob Girl from the student council meeting. And a few guys who seem to be refugees from the Starry Starry Night dance inside, ties flapping under their loosened collars, blazers, khakis—they look like baseball players, for sure, and as Jesse watches, they form a mini–mosh pit around Arlo, who hurls himself gleefully against and over them, his long, thin body flailing like a sock monkey tossed in a game of keep away.

A surprising number of teachers are here, too—not just Mr. Kennerley, who's been using StarMart as a case study in his social studies classes, but also Mr. Samms, the head of athletics, Ms. Speck from home ec, and Joe the special-ed aide who works one-on-one with Jamie, the mainstreamed kid with developmental delays. As she's watching, right in front of everybody, Joe dances casually by Mr. Samms, slides his hand lightly over his lower back, and kisses him lightly on the lips. It's brief and blasé, *so* no big deal, but still—Jesse blinks. Joe the special-ed guy and Mr. Samms? Everyone's coming out of the woodwork tonight.

A couple of little kids dart in and out of the crowd, chasing each other through the legs of the grown-ups. Huckle holds court on his back porch, passing out sodas and lazily kicking a hacky sack around with three or four other guys who look like they got lost on the way to a Phish concert.

In a corner of the fray, Margaret and Charlie sit side by side, like the king and queen of the dance. Bert, their Access-a-Ride driver, seems to have made a special off-hours run to bring them here this evening, and he stands behind the two of them, awkward and protective at the same time, like a Secret Service agent in his mirrored sunglasses. His arms are crossed high and tight over his chest, but Jesse notices that he's tapping his shiny patent-leather toe to the music.

In the middle of the dance floor, Fran and Arthur have their arms around each other, doing their three flashiest community-center-swing-dance-class moves over and over again. Normally, Jesse would be embarrassed to watch her pot-bellied, parka-wearing father dip her giggling mother to the floor. But Jesse hasn't seen them dance together like this for a long time, since before her mother got sick. It feels like a gift to see them so happy.

Someone's dog, a big, sleek, doleful-looking Weimaraner, threads its way through the crowd and out of the tent. Jesse is moving toward him to stroke his head when Emily appears beside her.

"Hi," Emily says tensely.

Emily is in an oversized overcoat—maybe Mike's—holding it closed with her clutched arms, but underneath Jesse can see a few inches of satiny blue party dress. She can only imagine what the rest of it looks like, what the shape of the neckline is, how the texture of that satin would feel on her fingers. She swallows, and extinguishes the thought.

"Hi," Jesse says. It's strange to be talking to Emily in public, even now, in the dark, this far away from other people.

"You're wearing it," Emily observes.

"What?" Jesse looks down at herself.

"Your, um, suit."

"Oh yeah."

"You wore it last year, too."

"I only wear it on special occasions," Jesse explains. "So, how's your dance going?"

"Incredible."

"How come you're not over there?"

Emily pauses. "I'm looking for Michael," she says. "Is he here?"

"I think he was. I think I saw him in there for a second." Jesse jerks her head toward the tent.

"He's in charge of my souvenir photo booth area. I left him and Snehal in charge, and I looked over a second ago and no one was manning it."

"Oh. I don't know if he's in there anymore. I haven't really been keeping track of who's been coming and going."

Emily looks past Jesse into the tent, and Jesse follows her gaze. The tent is hopping, but Mike doesn't seem to be there.

"Your dance is going great, too," Emily observes. Jesse starts to respond but Emily says suddenly, "I've been missing you."

"Oh." Jesse feels her heart lurch. She doesn't know how to respond.

Emily takes a step closer to her and lowers her voice a little.

"I think, you know, I think I was really stupid to say we shouldn't see each other anymore."

"Yeah?"

"Yeah. I don't know why I said it. I was so overwhelmed. I'm still really busy and overwhelmed but, like, it doesn't take any time away from my responsibilities to see you, right? It's just my break, it's easy to fit you in."

Jesse waits a second before she says, "Uh-huh."

"And I miss you. I actually miss you a lot. Can we forget I ever said that? Can we just, like, start up again on Tuesday?"

Jesse looks up at the night sky. Long, inky clouds are

streaked across it, but here and there, in between them, a scintillating diamond-point shines through.

"I don't know."

"Oh. You're too busy now?"

"No. I mean, I am, I'm busy, but I'm just not . . ." Jesse swallows. "I don't feel like hiding anymore."

"Oh."

Emily nods briskly. A shiver passes through her body, and she hugs herself, shrugs her shoulders up to her ears. Jesse fights the urge to wrap her arms around Emily, pull her close, keep her warm. She looks down at the ground.

"And I guess, like . . . I want to put my energy into other things?"

"Oh. Oh yeah." Emily nods again rapidly. "I get it. That's fine. I totally understand."

Jesse looks up and meets Emily's eye.

"But I still, like, love you," Jesse says, and Emily inhales sharply, like she might burst into tears.

For a moment, Jesse feels the energy wave encircle them once more, the one that draws them toward each other like ultra-magnetic gravitational pull. She feels it as fear this time: the sense that they're going to fall into each other, even if she doesn't want it to happen. If Emily says it back to her now, Jesse is afraid she'll give in to her completely.

But Emily doesn't say, "I love you, too." She says, "I'd better go find Michael," and she turns abruptly, and heads back across the parking lot toward the lit-up gym. After a couple of steps she breaks into a run.

Jesse stands and watches her go.

She's still watching when Esther appears, breathless, at Jesse's side.

"There you are!" Esther gasps. "I've been looking all over for you. Where have you been?"

Jesse says, "Here."

"Okay, well, can you come back under the tent? I left your mom in charge of the birdhouse–cash box, but I think she wants to get back up and dance."

"No, sure. Of course."

As Esther steers her in the direction of the tent, Jesse turns to look back over her shoulder at the parking lot. Emily's gone.

"It's crazy in there, isn't it?" Esther is practically bouncing up and down with excitement as she walks. "How many people do you think are here? Three hundred? Four hundred?"

"Um, more like seventy-five? But it's still great."

"The birdhouse–cash box is totally full," Esther gloats. "I had to take some money out to make room for more money." Jesse looks at Esther now and sees that she's a giddy, ecstatic mess—sweaty from dancing in her coat, her braids so undone that her hair is basically just a mass of curls with two vestigial rubber bands wadded up in it. In the distant glow of the lantern-tent, her eyes gleam.

"How much do you think we made so far?" Jesse asks.

"I don't know. Thousands. Millions." Esther giggles gleefully. "Can you believe how excellent this is?"

"It's awesome," Jesse agrees.

"It's paradise in there. And Arlo and Charlie are so happy. They have a whole crazy plan for what to do with the money. Apparently, they're going to start some kind of blog."

"Blogs are free."

"Yeah, I don't know, apparently they have some kind of big plan."

Jesse looks into the tent as they get closer to it, crowded with happy people bathed in yellow light. A little girl in a purple hat and coat has cuddled up with the Weimaraner, who is sitting, chin on paws, at the edge of the dance floor, and is sleeping on top of him. Arlo and the baseball players have stopped moshing, and Arlo is standing in the middle of them now, lecturing them animatedly about something (how to Dumpster-dive for fun and profit, no doubt) and making them all look at something on his BlackBerry.

"We made that," Esther says.

She reaches down and grabs Jesse's hand. In the cool night air, her hand is warm and dry, and her grip is strong.

Esther looks at Jesse admiringly. Under her gaze, Jesse feels her chin lift. She feels her shoulders straighten. She feels strong, and strange, and beautiful.

"Hey, you want to dance one dance before you take

over the birdhouse?" Esther suggests, tugging Jesse toward the tent. "Don't be scared. It's totally cool and non-gender-oppressive in there."

Esther pulls Jesse from the chilly dark into the warmth and noise and jostle of the dance floor. She takes hold of both of her hands, and spins her around like a little kid. They go faster and faster. Esther laughs. Jesse laughs. When Jesse looks up, the glittering lights of the tent blur above her like the stars of the universe.

THE ! ALL !! NEW!!!

SPANIFESTO

!!!!!!

providing you with

THREE

(3)

EASY STEPS TO
MAKE
THE WORLD
A BETTER PLACE

brought to you by

SPAN

The Student Peace Action Network

and

NOLAW

The National Organization
to Liberate All Weirdos

and their various

SUBSIDIARIES, COALITION MEMBERS,

disciples, acolytes, mentors,

dream dates, lovers, friends, former nemeses,

ex-girlfriends,

co-conspirators,

and

PARTNERS IN CRIME AND HARMONY.

STEP 1.

WHAT'S WRONG???

Name the problem. Identify the target.

STEP 2.

WHAT CAN YOU PERSONALLY DO TO MAKE IT BETTER???

You think a tiny step in the right direction is too small?

You're so wrong!!!

Every tiny step in the right direction

makes the world a tiny bit better.

WHO'S GONNA HELP YOU???

Alone you are one person.

You may be cute and interesting.

You may have lots of nice personality traits.

But you're solitary.

When you join up with

other

like-minded persons,

you become soldiers in an army.

Now you can be

UNSTOPPABLE.

So . . .

Who's going to work with you?

Who's going to donate money to you?

Who's going to listen to your

sometimes boring but always important

dreams?

Who's going to give you smart advice?

Who's going to dance with you all night long,

until the stars go out

and the sun comes up,

and you wake up into a brand-new morning where

your dreams,

no matter how optimistic,

have become real?

Have become the beautiful,

NEW

and

IMPROVED

version of the

world?????

Make a Difference

CONCERNED ABOUT SPRAWL?

READ:

Suburban Nation: The Rise of Sprawl and the Decline of the American Dream, by Andres Duany, Elizabeth Plater-Zyberk, and Jeff Speck. North Point Press, 10th anniversary edition, 2010.

WATCH:

The Corporation. Directed by Mark Achbar and Jennifer Abbot. 2003.

SEARCH FOR:

Big Box Tool Kit, from the Institute for Local Self-Reliance: www.bigboxtoolkit.com

CARE ABOUT QUEER KIDS?

READ:

GLBTQ: The Survival Guide for Gay, Lesbian, Bisexual, Transgender, and Questioning Teens, by Kelly Huegel. Free Spirit Publishing, second edition, 2011.

WATCH:

The Incredibly True Adventure of Two Girls in Love.
Directed by Maria Maggenti. 1995.

SEARCH FOR:

GLSEN, the Gay, Lesbian and Straight Education Network:
www.glsen.org

YouthResource, a website by and for lesbian, gay, bisexual,
transgender, and questioning young people: www.
amplifyyourvoice.org/youthresource

CURIOUS ABOUT JOAN?

READ:

Joan of Arc: Her Story, by Régine Pernoud and Marie-
Véronique Clin. Translated by Jeremy duQuesnay Adams.
St. Martin's Press, 1998.

The Story of Joan of Arc, by Maurice Boutet de Monvel
and Gerald Gottlieb. Dover, 2010.

WATCH:

The Passion of Joan of Arc. Directed by Carl Theodor
Dreyer. 1928.

SEARCH FOR:

International Joan of Arc Society: smu.edu/ijas

Acknowledgments

Thank you Joy Peskin, the wisest, kindest, fiercest, smartest, most patient, most uncompromising, funniest editor a writer could have.

Thank you Kendra Levin, the Story Whisperer.

Thank you Janet Pascal and Susan Jeffers, astute, assiduous, astonishingly knowledgeable copyeditors.

Thank you Merrilee Heifetz, superagent.

Thank you Katie George and Steve George, Jenny George and Kate Carr, wonderful family.

Thank you 13P, New Dramatists, New York Writers Coalition, and Brooklyn Writers Collaborative, support networks and inspiration sources.

Thank you Matt Longabucco and Carley Moore, best friends and favorite poets.

Thank you Malka Longabucco, curiosity engine, speed demon, comedian.

Thank you Lisa Kron, brave, brilliant, beautiful, beloved.